Fallen Flower, Fragrant Grass

An Anthology of Life Stories

Vishy Sankara

ISBN 979-8-89906-755-6

Epigraph

All beings by nature are Buddha,

As ice by nature is water.

Apart from water there is no ice,

Apart from beings, no Buddha.

How sad that people ignore the near

and search for truth afar.

Like someone in the midst of water

crying out in thirst.

……… …………………………………………

At this moment what are you seeking?

Nirvana is right here before your eyes.

This very place is the Lotus Land!

This very body, the Buddha!

– The Song of Zazen *(Hakuin Zenji)*

Dedication

There were three Sankaras in my life...

EMS, Sankara and Adi Sankara.

Of the three, it was Sankara, my late father,

who taught me without teaching me

to walk on the Middle Way between left and right.

I dedicate this book to his wonderful memories.

Contents

Foreword: Blessing on the Way...

Viswanathan Sankara has gathered in this book form some of his reflections. They are not mere theories or exhortations. They are his life experiences. He has traveled widely and has had multifarious experiences. Especially, I liked very much his experience in the "Arabian desert in the moonlight under the starry sky above, pregnant with unspeakable silence." Silence becomes his very self and also his teacher.One can remember the psalm, "Be still and know that I am God." The Latin poet Terence expressed it as: "Homo sum, humani nihil a me alienum puto," meaning: "I am human and nothing human is alien to me."

Vishy, as he popularly known, combines his life experiences with zen insights. It is an invitation to others to taste zen realisation. Vishy is a studious student of zen. I am happy with his commitment and seriousness. He is willing to let go of all his worldly ambitions and possessions and devote himself solely to the study and realisation of zen. It is rare to find such people. I think he will go far in the zen journey. As a bodhisattva, he can help many and show them the path of liberation and freedom.

I bless him and wish him well in his journey.

Fr. AMA Samy, Zen Master

Bodhi Sangha

https://kanzeonzendo.in

Prologue: An Egg Song

**A proem to "Fallen Flower,
Fragrant grass"**

This is My Egg Song.

If you are wondering what an "egg song" is, let me explain. It's the celebratory crackle from mother hen when she lays an egg—a proud proclamation of her achievement. Often the other hens join the celebration and create quite a symphony, or a cacophony if you will. Either way, it's a moment of collective celebration. I kind of believe I've earned my own Egg Song too!

Look at the numbers. As of 2023, the International Standard Book Number (ISBN) estimates there are roughly 158,464,880 unique books in the world. And that's just the published ones! If you add blogs, manuscripts, and all the other writings, it's easy to believe that there are probably more writers than readers today. In such a crowded space, a writer's Egg Song becomes essential—a small crackle to grab some time and mindshare from you, my readers.

From Ancient Scrolls to Modern Scribbles

The oldest printed book, *The Diamond Sutra*, was printed in China way back in 868 AD and it remains one of the most revered Buddhist texts. Dated even before that is the *Epic of Gilgamesh*, the oldest surviving written literature. It is from ancient Mesopotamia and is often considered to be the first great literary composition. Back then, I'm pretty sure authors didn't need to sing Egg Songs. Take Buddha, for instance. He never had to market or sell his sutras. From kings to paupers, people were all ears whenever the Enlightened One spoke.

However, **I'm no Buddha and I do need an Egg Song**. Why? Because, by all modern standards, I'm nothing extraordinary. I am not much of a writer, let alone an accomplished author! I'm an ordinary mind in an ordinary form, living an ordinary life. Yet, herein lies the twist. It was quite an aha moment in my life when I learnt from my **Zen Master AMA Samy**—after a number of Zazens, Dokusans for Kōans and teishos—that, in the Zen Way, an ordinary mind and an ordinary life have a greater significance; these attributes transcend the noisy accolades of modern life.

A Tale of Two Great Influences: Kumaran Asan and AMA Samy

The title of my book is a tribute to two great influences: **Kumaran Asan**, the celebrated Malayalam poet, and my Zen Master, **AMA Samy**. Kumaran Asan is the most read, discussed and famous poet of Malayalam literature. As one of the foremost disciples and close confidants of Sri Narayana Guru, he was much more than a poet. He was a spiritual and social thinker and his poems had deep spiritual, philosophical and social underpinnings.

Veena Poovu (*The Fallen Flower*) is his most famous and widely read poem. He wrote the poem when he was taking care of his ailing Guru in Palakkad, which also happens to be my home town! I first read *Veena Poovu* when I was a 9th standard student at KTM High School in Mannarkkad. Our teacher, Kumaran Master, had a magical way of teaching poetry and the poignant verses etched themselves in my mind. Incidentally, our teacher's son Manoj Kumar was my classmate then, and continues to be my good friend now. In fact, he is the current headmaster of the same school!

Veena Poovu is the story of a flower that has fallen to the ground and is lying, seemingly unwanted. The great poet uses the poem as a metaphor for the transient nature of our lives. A flower that was once admired and sought after—whether as an offering to a deity, or to adorn a woman's hair—now lay on the ground, half decayed and on its way to merge with mother earth. The poem mirrors the phases of our own life: birth, youth, glory, death, and decay.

Years later, as I walked the Zen way under AMA Samy, I stumbled upon his book titled *Falling Blossoms and Fragrant Grass*. The title triggered my memories of my 9th standard Malayalam class. The book reconnected me to *Veena Poovu* and I revisited the poem after four decades. This time I saw it with new eyes. I realised it was a sobering reminder of impermanence, a truth beautifully aligned with Buddhist philosophy. Yes, the flower falls, it decays. But as AMA Samy's book reminded me, **even a fallen flower can spread its fragrance before it returns to the earth.**

My Fragrant Scribbles

This anthology—a collection of blogs or mental scribbles, as I like to call them—spans 15 years of my life. It's a reflection of who I am: a fallen flower, perhaps, but one that still strives to leave behind a bit of fragrance. I am here, still trying to do some good in this beautiful world before I, too, return to Mother Earth.

So dear reader, this is my Egg Song—a small crackle of celebration for my offering.

I hope you hear it. I hope it lingers.

Love, Peace and Joy.

Chapter 1

Monsoon @ Mannarkkad: Rainmaker of Joy and Peace

7 April 2024

"Can you remember who you were, before the world told you who you should be?"

– Charles Bukowski

This thought-provoking quote by Charles Bukowski captures the essence of finding our true self. It is quite possible that an early childhood event—which could sometimes be a slightly traumatic one, as in my case—shapes and makes "I/me" and guides and navigates our thoughts and responses to the world in general, to ourselves in particular. It loses its stranglehold on us only when we become aware of it and realise how it has shaped our life so far. It is from that eureka moment that we can start working on our psyche and soul to reclaim our original self.

My reclaim-myself-mission was triggered in 2002 when Dr. Richard McHugh picked me as a volunteer for a timeline exercise in his NLP class. It took me some 21years to complete that mission as a Zen student of Fr. Ama Samy. When Dr. McHugh did that exercise with me, that bitter sweet childhood event played out vividly in my mind, like a multi colour cinema scope movie. Now when I try to recollect that event, it appears like a hazy black and white reel, soundless and quite detached. In NLP parlance, I am quite done with it.

The way our brain amplifies or diminishes our experiences in our memories, through the process of generalisation, deletion and distortion, based on our perspective of the event, is quite amazing. A few weeks ago, I facilitated the same NLP timeline exercise with one of my coachee. She could remember many sorrowful experiences in her timeline very vividly while the joyful ones were few and far between. Interestingly, while she recollected those events, she was still attached to the sad events. She could still see the events unfolding, unlike her happy moments in life.

Coming Back to My Own Road to Damascus....

I was all of four and a half years old then, and quite a handful. I am absolutely sure about my age. It might have been the last week of May or very early June. Our ALP School had not opened yet but the monsoon was about to start. My parents advanced my date of birth on record so that the naughty troublemaker would not be at home, at least during school hours!

One evening, one of my uncles—who had then recently graduated and was job hunting—stepped out of the house for his evening outing with his friends. He said something to my brother and me, and I replied to him. I must have said something quite disrespectful since it triggered in him one of those outlier reactions of anger and violence. Though there are always enough small sticks lying around a Kerala home to deal with a small brat, he chose to discipline a four-and-half year old by folding a steel wire used to dry clothes and used that as his bata sćoir. That was the worst thrashing I got in my life. Never before and never after. So far at least! My poor mother tried to stop it, but without much success. After my uncle left, she just held on to me and tried to stop my sobbing. I guess she herself was crying.

That is when the monsoon rains arrived that year and wiped my tears away. Traditional Kerala houses have these long verandhas with wooden benches and wide wooden balustrades all around the house. The houses are kind of half open to the world and nature.

When it rains, one can sit on a bench, resting one's chin on the wooden balustrade and watch the rain for hours. As the direction of the rain changes with the wind, one gets needle showers on the face too. It is quite hypnotic and can take one to another world altogether. It ended up being an anchor of joy and peace for me. There is a Zen kōan that says,"Blood cannot wash away blood, and thoughts can't save you from more thoughts," but I can tell you from my experience that raindrops from heaven can wipe away tears of the heart.

That was my first memory of the magic of monsoon rains, my first and original psychotherapist.

The Therapeutic Monsoon Rains

Nothing in this world nourishes and refreshes the thirsty, parched and sun-baked earth as the monsoon rain. It is impossible to not like almost everything about the rain...the fresh smell of earth, the rhythmic beats as it pours down on those Mangalore tiles, the small icy pellets of new rain and the feeling of it on summer skin rashes, the taste of black coffee and the crispiness of jackfruit papad!

It offers the same therapeutic massage to hurting hearts too. It often starts with darkness, even at noon. Then absolute silence after the birds scurry back to their nests indicating that the curtain is going to rise for the light and sound show of nature's orchestra in God's own country.

The Turning Point

A little later my father came home from office and saw my plight. That was the end of joint family life for us. There is a Zen kōan parody, "How many drops of susu does it take to spoil a broth of soup?" The usual answer is one. That is applicable to family, community, organisations and countries.

Not long after that, we moved out of our family home in the small town of Mannarkkad and relocated to a tiny village called Thenkara.

Although the distance between the two places was just 5 km, it was a kind of time travel to the past. To start with, Thenkara had no electricity yet, it reached the village three-four years after we moved there. School was a good 2–2.5 km away. There were less than five small shops in the village. And there were probably just four-five buses plying through the village each day. And most interestingly, the *Mathrubhumi* newspaper reached us only after 9 am! And in Kerala, that is a measure of progress of a place.

The Joys of Thenkara

But the experience of rain just got better. While Mannarkkad translates to soil + river + forest, Thenkara in Malayalam means shore of honey. A land of fragrant grasses and falling blossoms. It is located en route to the Silent Valley National Park and we had moved a little closer to it. Anamooli, meaning where the elephants hum, is about 2 km away from Thenkara. Meanwhile, we lived in a small house located atop a small hill. There were no walls or fences or a gate in front of the house. Rain, joy and peace visited cheerfully—unhindered and undeterred. There were two small waterfalls nearby and we could hear the roar of one but strangely, I don't remember ever seeing the waterfalls.

We had many friends in the neighbourhood. Though many of them had to do chores at home and in the fields, there were plenty of playmates all around. And topping all of them was an Akshaya Patra kind of jackfruit tree behind our house. It bore the tastiest jackfruits we had had in our lives! It took care of the jackfruit needs of not only our home, but also all the other homes in the neighbourhood and countless birds and squirrels. My mother made sure we spent our summer vacations making tons and tons of jackfruit papad to ensure an endless supply of monsoon snacks for her three children. And we worked like squirrels collecting nuts!

Over time life took me to places I had never dreamt of. I experienced rains in Bangalore, Mumbai, Germany, England, USA, Oman, South Africa and even Saudi Arabia. But none had the charm of monsoon rains at Mannarkkad, those foreign rains smelt and tasted nothing like my childhood monsoons. These rains were kind of half hearted, more like insipid bathroom showers.

Monsoon While at Poomully Mana

Over a decade ago, in June of 2012, I was the only inpatient or resident at the Poomully Ayurveda Mana Treatment Centre for more than two weeks. It was one of those serendipitous moments in my life. During those times, I was kind of living a life of exile in the deserts of the Middle East. It takes time to get used to the endless expanses of sand and to begin seeing its beauty. At least, it took me quite a while. As I was warned not to write any blogs there, the only way to retain a semblance of sanity was to read and listen to music. The book *Poomully AramThamburan* by writer, actor and TV anchor V K Sriraman, was one of the books I happened to read there. Poomully Mana is quite well known in the Malabar region. Poomully Mana—Mana is a Nampoothiri family home—has a history of more than 500 years. The members of Poomully Mana were famous as practitioners and experts of ayurveda, vedas, yoga, kalari (martial-art) and music. When I enquired about their ayurvedic treatment, I was told that due to some legal disputes between the partners, they had closed it down. But a few weeks later, they called me and asked to come over. And that's how I ended up as a lone resident in that ancient mana for two weeks during the monsoon.

The resident doctor would visit twice a day with home made medicines. The ayurvedic treatment usually ended during the morning hours. And a staff member would come with food and also work as a security guard for the night. During most of my time there, I would be sitting on that cane chair, reading and looking at the sky waiting for the rain. It was quite dramatic, the way the monsoon arrived. It usually started late at noon. Darkness at noon! Absolute silence before the light and sound show of nature's orchestra in God's own country.

Even in that storm, an old lady would come and light a few lamps in that old dilapidated temple in front of the mana.That was my first course of ayurvedic treatment. While the medicines, the strict disciplined diet (read starving) cured my physical body, the monsoon rain did wonders to my heart and soul.

Back to the beginning!

Soon after, I left my corporate job and took a plunge into the unknown. After almost a Jupiter cycle of life with some struggle, some smiles, some tears, some sorrow, some pain and some gain, I find myself once again at the same four-way junction in my life. And that kind of points to the fact that I still have work to do, to reclaim myself from myself, regardless of the number of days at Zendo, the minutes of Zazen and the number of kōans.

And this May/June I plan to go to Perumalmalai to be one with the monsoon rains and myself. I may not have to go all the way back to Thenkara to find it, like Santiago, Paul Coelho's hero in Alchemist.

Chapter 2

Dutching Synergy the Tiki-Taka Way

11 July 2010

I started drafting this post in my mind while watching the Holland-Uruguay World Cup match. During the final phase, Dutch star Arjen Robben was substituted and the camaraderie shown by the Holland bench was quite striking, especially if you are aware of their history. Despite its small size and population, Holland has always produced a remarkable bunch of soccer players, particularly during the 70s and 90s. I remember their 90s lineup well: Gullit, Rijkaard, Van Basten, Bergkamp, the De Boer brothers, and other worthy players.

They had the world at their feet, but a few disruptive elements in the team always ensured they did not click as a unit. During one of the group matches of the current World Cup, when Van \ was substituted, he had a few words of advice for the coach in front of millions of viewers. A commentator, who lipread Van Persie, mentioned that he was abusing his own teammate, Sneijder. I thought history was repeating itself, the Dutch way. But for once, the coach was wise. He took the initiative to bring the conflict out in the open, and the players spoke to each other. And for a change, the Dutch ended up in the finals.

May be it was a coincidence. The next day, I attended—as an observer—a training program on synergy conducted by an esteemed colleague. Quite remarkably, he started with a question: what has made Dhoni's Indian cricket team such a success? The answer was obvious: Synergy.

I thought the word was quite self explanatory. Synergy = Synchronised Energy. Synchronised means harmonised. As in a laser beam. After all, a laser beam is nothing but coherent light. Of course, the coherence is enforced by an external source of energy and process; it is not an intrinsic quality of light.

That night, Spain pushed Germany out of the park the Tiki-Taka way. Tiki-Taka refers to the style of football played by FC Barcelona and the current Spain World Cup football team. It is a short passing game, where everyone in the team participates and weaves magic around the rival team. It is quite common for them to conjure a sequence of 25+ passes before putting the ball in the net. It takes sublime skills and innate understanding of the other players to play the Tiki-Taka way. Incidentally, this way of playing was said to be the brainchild of Johan Cruyff, the greatest Dutch footballer.He probably realised that the Dutch might not adopt his style, so he took it to Barcelona. No wonder, seven players from Barcelona were in the starting lineup for Spain.

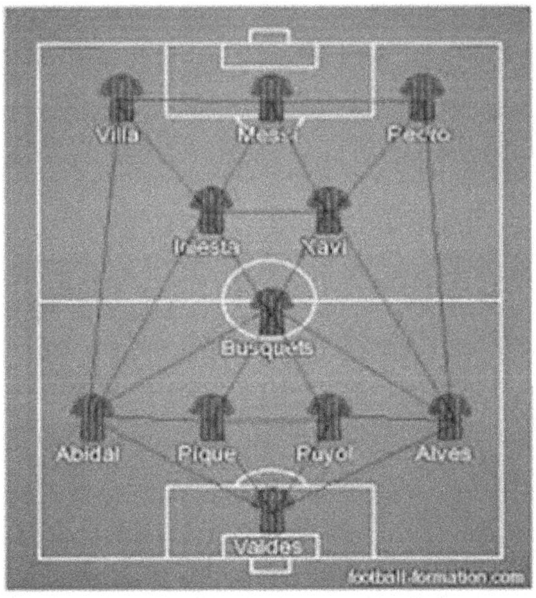

FC Barcelona Tiki Taka Formation Courtesy: https://blogs.cornell.edu/ info2040/2014/09/18/fc-barcelona-and-the-triadic-closure-property/

The "facility-trainer" in the synergy training session told us that the crux of having synergy is not knowing how to do it, but having a strong reason for doing it! As an old saying goes - if your why is strong enough, you will figure out how. It is the common answer to the question "Why" that sublimates individual egos and forges synergy.

The final game starts in another 30 minutes. Johan Cruyff, the Dutch great has predicted a Spanish win. I am also pitching for La Roja.

The Dutch can wait till they learn to play the Tiki-Taka way.

(This blog was written on 12 July 2010 as I was waiting for the World Cup final match to start. I called it right. :-))

Chapter 3

6 Feet Down Under

4 December 2024

"Every man's life ends the same way, it is only the details of how he lived and how he died that distinguishes one man from another."

– Ernest Hemingway in "For Whom the Bell Tolls"

Thus wrote Ernest Hemingway in his answer to Leo Tolstoy's *War and Peace* titled *"For whom the bell tolls"*.

My eyes were moist, my mind blank, as I stood holding an ancient and rusted iron gate that was locked with chain and lock as if they did not want their dead and buried to walk back to this world. As the great Moroccan traveler Ibn Battutah had written

"Travelling at first leaves you speechless, then turns you into a storyteller. Travelling at the speed of light, through mountains and valleys of memories in our mind is no different."

– Ibn Battutah, the great Moroccan traveler

I was trying to locate the spot where my late father Sankara was taking his last rest. After the monsoon, Kerala homes with a backyard often become a forest and people have to clear the dense foliage to keep snakes and wild animals out of their backyard.

Besides my father, my uncle, their cousins, grandparents, great grandparents, other blood relatives and generations of our ancestors too share that social space. It covers an acre of land on the border of the perennial evergreen Kunthipuzha river, which originates in the Silent Valley and flows into the Arabian Sea. And that piece of land is the best, most beautiful and serene spot for eternal rest. Graves here are not marked as this is a common burial ground of the Kannadigas of Mannarkkad. Only the living draw boundaries and worry about what they own, after death and before birth, everything belongs to everyone. Another common thread between all people resting there is, their love of that river. During the monsoon, when she overflows and carries with her everything from elephants to a few humans to the Arabian sea, the river becomes quite mild mannered after the rainy seasons. I am sure the hoary tunes of the river sound like lullabies to them. And in the overpopulated and overcrowded state of Kerala, an acre of such land is precious. It is quite a luxury that the Kannadigas of Mannarkkad, who included only around ten homes, had their own burial ground. We would call our community "Athatti" (meaning ten households in Kannada, although now it has come down to just two or three).

My father fought against a local wealthy strongman who tried to take over the piece of land with the connivance of a distant relative of ours. Sankara was a lifelong cardholding member of CPI and he could walk into the offices of ministers and leaders of the Left. My heart would swell with pride pride and joy, when they received him with so much respect and affection. When K E Ismail, was revenue minister of Kerala my father got him to instruct our Collector to issue an order that handed over the title of that land within a day. Perhaps that was my father's way of ensuring that greedy strangers with dubious values couldn't encroach and disturb his last slumber.

I left that place mentally the moment my dear dad was buried. And I was back there after 18years! I was at Mannarkkad to attend the diamond jubilee celebrations of my high school KTMHS. It was the alma mater of my father Sankara too.

Kunthipuzha river at Mannarkkad

As I was planning to leave home and move to a Zendo, I thought I should talk to him and seek his blessings. Though 18 years is along time, and his physical remains would have gone back to mother earth 6 feet under. Suddenly that phrase 6 feet under stuck in my head. It sounds like a softened phrase for a grave or burial ground, or more generally for death.

As Hemingway wrote, every man's life does not end in the same way. Some are buried, some are cremated, some are left for a sky burial (though the dwindling population of vultures have now forced the Parsis to choose either cremation or burial, some choose to leave their dead bodies as learning material at medical colleges. In fact I have chosen that option and mentioned it in my will. Some bury their dead in the sea like the US Navy. Osama bin Laden's body was also thrown in the sea so that the burial place could not become a shrine. King Abdullah the previous king of the Kingdom of Saudi Arabia was buried in an unmarked grave for the same reason. Mughal emperors built their burial sites so that they remain marked in history and geography. While some like Akbar did it with class, Shajahan did a crass job by building a monument, the construction of which inflicted great pain on those who built it and the economy as well.

Perhaps they all wanted their mortal remains to be treated just the way they lived on earth. Some lightly, like birds in the sky and some like tyrants, they lived just 6 feet above all, their concerns and fears about what would happen to them when they are dead and gone.

From time immemorial, ever since the first generation of human beings started living on earth, the challenges of day-to-day living took the lion's share of their concerns and mindspace. But their fears and concerns about death, dying and what would happen to them defined the way they lived. All philosophy and religions etc. might have originated from this fear more than anything else.

Even someone like Jiddu Krishnamurti, who spoke to many audiences over a long lifetime on conditioning of the mind was not fully free from this, in my view. I had read that during his last days at Ojai, when it was clear to him and everyone else that his end was imminent, he instructed others to contact the pandits of Varanasi to find out how an enlightened man or saint should be cremated, and then exclaimed over what he was doing! But then again, he instructed his trustees that the electric crematorium chamber had to be cleaned thoroughly before they placed his mortal remains inside it. He did not want his ashes to be contaminated by another's human's ashes!

A long time ago, during an interaction with some trustees of the KFI on conditioned minds, I had shared this nugget of information with great enthusiasm. One of the trustees, an absolutely brilliant man, who chose to join a KFI school after his graduation from IIMC strongly put me in my place, directing me not to share unfounded stories and said that he had been present at Ojai at that time. I kept my silence. Not for too long though. I came back home, took out biographies written by May Lutyens and others and emailed him the information keying in those pages and references. He was a thorough gentleman and quite humble. He did reply with an apology.

The whole point of sharing this is point out that, even a great philosopher like Krishnamurti was still struggling with his conditioned thoughts about the end of life.

While I was struggling with kōan number 14 from *Mumonkan (The Gateless Gate), Nansen Kills the cat,* Fr AMA Samy told me "I die and I don't die. I don't die so that I can die". Accept death. Act as if I am dying was the answer to that koan. As Joshu would have told his Zen master Nansen, "Master, you can kill, but can you give life ?"

In Zen, there is no distinction between life and death, which is viewed as part of a continuum with life. Both life and death are one and the same and there is no dividing line. As per Zen, what we think as a person, is an ongoing process and not a product. And when we let go of our illusory sense of self, we lose our fear of death. The only way to know life is to be aware of living, because life is now and this is the only gateless gate to cross.

Chapter 4

Mountain, Desert and Metaphors for Change!

11 August 2024

"How big is the top of Mount Everest?"

"About the size of a small kitchen table," he responded. "That is amazing," I said, "You know, when you cross the SaharaDesert, there is no way of knowing where the desert ends. There is no peak, no border, no sign that says, 'You are now leaving the Sahara Desert – Have a niceDay!'"

– From Steve Donahue's "Shifting Sands:
A Guidebook for Crossing
the Deserts of Change".

Metaphors not only run our life, but they also reveal our thoughts; they liberate as well as imprison our minds. Case in point—after returning from a pilgrimage to Sabarimala as a young child, I became enamoured by Eknath Easwaran's spiritual classic, *Climbing the Blue Mountain* and Jack Krakauer's *Into Thin Air*. Mountains became etched in my mind as a metaphor for a summit, spiritual or any human endeavour.

All of it Changed in a Moment Under the Desert Sky

About 12 years ago, on a fine day, I landed at Lekhwair Airport inOman. The airport was located on the edge of the vast Empty Quarter (Rub'al-Khali in Arabic), a sand desert covering around 650,000 square kilometres. It covers a huge part of Saudi Arabia, UAE, Yemen and Oman. It is about 1,000 km long and 500 km wide. It has reddish orange sand dunes that can reach up to 250 m.

Our team included Gabriel Bennet, Said, Rukmuddin Khan and I. We were part of a team working on a transformation project for PDO, Oman. My role was that of a change and transformation consultant. Rukmuddin was our system architect. Said, who was from Syria, had worked as a petroleum engineer for about three decades and was our SME. Gab, our project manager, was a die-hard football and Barcelona fan. Fieldwork for the project took us to almost all oil fields of PDO. And that is why we landed at Lekhwair PDO Airport too.

Lekhwair camp is quite far from the airport. The driver of the Landcruiser jeep who took us to the PDO camp, was a long-time employee at PDO. He also happened to be a native of Kerala and needless to say, we bonded quite well. In fact, his home in Kerala was not too far from the place I belonged to. He told us that he would drive us to the desert one evening. He said the desert was worth visiting, especially on a full moon night.

On the next full moon night, he drove us quite close to the point where the borders of Saudi Arabia, UAE and Oman meet. As the lights of the camp faded behind us, we were almost amid the vastness of the desert. And then the jeep came to a halt. Suddenly we all became silent as we stepped out into the desert. The reddish orange colour of the sand glistened under the full moonlight. And it was one of those moments when the universe came to a standstill for me. Truly a blessed moment. The light and shade artwork crafted by the moonlight on the sides of sand dunes, the mixed colours on the horizon, the clear sky shimmering with shy stars and a brazen full watt moon. It was magical. All of us just dissolved into it.

Photo Courtsey: Freepik

I can now confidently say, that was the moment that triggered my love for the desert. And books of Thesiger, Antoine de Saint-Exupéry,

Steve Donahue etc. took over my bookshelf. *Arabian Sands*; *Shifting Sands*; *Wind, Sand and Stars* are all classic must-reads. Until then the only book on Arabia I had read was *The Arabian Nights*. But then that book was about Aladdin, Sindbad and others more than about the sand and its beauty. Benyamin and *Goat Days* came much later.

The wonderful book, *Shifting Sands: A Guidebook for Crossing the Deserts of Change*, rewrote all my previously held textbook concepts about organisational transformation and change. All those theories that were cast in stone, were in reality cookie cutter solutions. That book reoriented my focus on the uniqueness of a context and people in it. From then on, it became more about transformation of people in a particular context and much less about what we mandate as change. Ever since, that compass has been holding good for me, from personal change—self, children, dear and near—to coachee, to organisations to ecosystems.

A long time ago, as a member of an ad hoc committee of a residential apartment complex, I remember sharing with other teammates, who were all super achievers in their respective fields, this principle. Every organisation and group of people differ. Army, corporations and commercial entities, a club, a cricket team. When we carry our baggage of success in one scenario to another, without making necessary changes in our mindset, our effectiveness as change catalysts gets impacted drastically.

Coming Back to the First Thought

All these thoughts and memories rushed through my mind, as I was looking at the screen with the picture of the mountain. There were three labels on that mountain: now, next year and later. And our president (ICF Bangalore Chapter) was talking about our organisation's plan for next year.

How do I work with my own teenage sons—Manu and Rishi are vastly different in their mindset, temperament and the way they look at the world—or my colleagues at work or my coachee (paid, pro bono and low-bono)? What about Bodhi Sangha members?

Do I really practice what I learned? Or in the madness to catch up with time, I assume, "What is good for the goose is good for the gander as well?"

Early this morning, I was searching for my old notes on that book. And here it is, the summary of summaries.

The title of the note was/is, "How do you navigate in the shifting sands of desert of change?" The note was ten years old and dated 7-Jan-2014. Now, ten years down the lane of life, I see the rate of change has increased exponentially.

While we are busy planning for yesterday, tomorrow is already knocking on our door. Still, be still for a moment or two. Don't rush in. The solution is not to skydive right into it with our cookie cutter solutions. Remember the proverb, fools rush in where angels fear to tread. Then there's Festina Lente, or make haste very slowly. This should be our unchanging motto as change catalysts. There was a famous quote from Einstein, "If I have one hour to solve a problem, I will spend 50 minutes trying to understand the problem." That holds good in our missions of change as well. Whether we are working with a coachee, a family, a project, an organisation or ourselves. Work on learning about the context and the lives in it.

And here is a Summary of the Above Note.

Metaphors are symbols of effort, achievement, journey, win, loss and even life. They offer lessons such as…

- It is important to be aware of the terrain.

- What works on Mt. Everest is useless in the Sahara.

- In the desert's scorching and shifting sands, wearing stiff alpine boots or plotting a start-to-finish route spells trouble.

- Follow a compass, not a map. In the desert, a map is worthless. A compass, however, functions without fail. In the deserts of life, you must learn to follow your own compass, which is an innermost sense of purpose and direction.

- Lower your gaze. In the desert, looking ahead to the horizon is defeating. It never gets any closer.

- Stop pushing. In the Sahara, it's pointless to push a car that's stuck in the sand. Instead, you deflate the tires and that lifts the vehicle up and out of the sand. In the deserts of life, it's pointless to keep pushing when you're in a rut. Instead, deflate your own ego or stubbornness.

- Know when to duck. In the Sahara, it's okay to duck. If your camel walks under a low-hanging branch, why not dodge the blow? In the deserts of life, it's okay to avoid a hit you're not ready for.

Acknowledgement: Sincere thanks to Sir Wilfred Thesiger (Mubarak bin London), Steve Donahue, Sir Edmond Hilary and Jon Krakauer for their wonderful ideas.

Books: *Arabian Sands* and *Into Thin Air*

Pause for a moment

Now, what is your context of change? Is it still a mountain, desert, river, or canyon? Or an urban apartment complex? Or is it an AI startup? Please don't rush in with a plan and solution. Pause for a moment.

Chapter 5

On D(th)e Motivation

22 August 2024

Recently, I found myself slipping on the proverbial thin ice and fell into a book writing project. Though I am a bibliophile and my literary idols, such as O. V. Vijayan, rank far above SachinTendulkar in my personal list, I never saw myself becoming an author. I didn't want to belong to any particular class of writers, more so after seeing some rather crass characters trying to crash the party with grandiose claims.

However, as I dusted myself off, I realised Idid not want to change my mind for two compelling reasons.

The minor reason: One of the few things I really love in life is sitting at my desk not doing anything. Yes, NOTHING. Then comes reading, and writing follows as a close third in my list.

The major reason: The person I'm collaborating with on this project is quite interesting. He carries his impressive achievements in academics, his professional life and social service quite lightly. His amiable nature and humility anchor him firmly to the ground.

Together, we decided to write on the themes of demotivation and motivation—topics that resonate deeply with both of us.

Photo courtesy: Linkedin https://www.linkedin.com/pulse/every-employees-journey-motivated-demotivated-sayed-mahmoud-phr-mba/

The path forward was not smooth. I struggled as usual in a Dante-esque hell of indecision and made painfully slow progress over the next three to four months. As I really started to live up to one of my lowest scoring traits as per Harrison Assessment—the tendency to be eager and excited about one's own goals—Pandit Ravi Shankar passed away. No, I am not a great fan of the sitar or of classical music, but the incident triggered certain memories.

A Slight Digression: Hikari Ōe's Story

I have to digress a bit here. During the Christmas and New Year holidays of 1998, I was in West Haven, Connecticut, and working in nearby Fairfield, not far from Sandy Hook, infamous for the recent shooting massacre. One of the most memorable books I read during that time was *The Music of Light*, a biography of Hikari Ōe, the eldest son of Kenzaburō Ōe, the Nobel Prize-winning Japanese author. When Hikari was born, he was described as a "monster baby" with a portion of his brain exposed. Doctors advised Kenzaburō to let the newborn die, predicting a life of immense struggle and social stigma in post-war Japan. They added that the complex operation to remove the protruding brain had very little chance of success.

But when Kenzaburō returned from a writing assignment in Hiroshima, he found his son still alive. The attitude of the victims of the atomic bomb, who had every reason to kill themselves but bravely wanted to live on, shamed him. Ōe demotivated himself from the thoughts of the passive death of his son, the fear, self doubt and bondage, and chose surgery, life, freedom and a somewhat uncertain future. The doctors removed the protruding part of the brain and with it went 70 percent of the baby's vision and ability to speak. In fact, Hikari seemed to be absolutely unaware of the world around him. And the first voice the boy responded to was that of a chirping bird.

At the age of six, Hikari spoke to his father while the two of them were in the woods. Let me quote from the book. "That is a water rail," said Hikari. When Ōe reported the incident to the family physician, he told Ōe that many retarded children were skilled mimics and could repeat complex sounds and messages without any understanding of what they were saying. Undaunted, Ōe and his wife introduced Hikari to music. The results were astonishing. Not only could Hikari recognise individual compositions, but he also began to request his favourites. "Play Chopin!" he would say, or even, "Play the second movement of Beethoven's Third Symphony." Hikari spent his days lying at his father's feet, listening to classical music. Then, he began to draw lines on paper and told his father that he was writing music. The doting father employed a tutor who taught

Hikari the musical scale, and Hikari's music began to resemble "real music." Then, the inevitable happened. A musician took the boy's music home and played it! Again, the verdict was predictable. Hikari was mimicking music that he had heard, said the doctors. Certainly he was not *composing*! But he was. At the time Hikari's daytime routine included attending a sheltered workshop where he assembled clothes pens, and no, he wasn't very good at it. After countless evaluations, and at the urging of his musical friends, Ōe decided to record his son's music. Concerned that the recording would be a financial disaster, Ōe offered to buy 200 copies of the CD, *The Music of Hikari Ōe*. However, upon the release of the CD, it immediately became a bestseller. So far, the CD has sold over 1 million copies and has now reached the United States. A second CD has since been completed. The music is described as "pure, innocent, and painfully beautiful."

Coming Back...

But then this story is not about Hikari; it's about demotivation. While Kenzaburo could demotivate his "manimal" attitude, the killer of Sandy Hook could not. Neither could the brutal "manimals" of Delhi.

Truth be told, it's a mistake to label the cruel behaviour we exhibit as animalistic and kindness as humane. It's true that the human race began its race towards civilisation and cultured behaviour a few thousands years ago only but animals have been on Mother Earth for millions of years. While animals instinctively fight for their food, lives and territory, it is the thinking part of the brain of man that has made him brutal, cruel and insensitive.

Perhaps all the gods, systems and tools our ancestors invented were to demotivate and curb the darker parts of our brain so that we could fit into society and maintain some amount of harmony. A good person is aware of the bad within and tries to demotivate and neutralise it, while a bad person remains oblivious. It's in the demotivation and elimination of the bad that the good can truly survive.

The Age of the Human Brain

Most of what we know about our brains has been learnt over the last couple of decades. It is important to understand that the age of our brain is way beyond our physical age. Our brains were not created in just the eight to nine months we spent in our mother's womb. Each one of us has inherited the evolution of the brain, over thousands of years, from the first human couple in Ethiopia, Africa. Or maybe even from them. Many programs in our brain are kind of hardwired from nature. And then through nurture to some extent, we reprogram it.

We are all endowed with a list of wonderful traits along with some not so great traits. The current model of the brain proposed by the scientific world is that of a modular brain. Neuroscientists seem to be moving away from the triune model of the brain. To put it in simple terms, many of the programs in our brain that keep us functioning, map across different regions of the brain. It is very possible that two programs are in complete conflict with each other and fighting it out to get through to the command center of action, reaction and response.

Thoughts Think Us

It is also interesting to note that the new model is in tune with what Buddha had tried to teach us about our mind. The fact that thoughts think us and not the other way, is a humbling learning for our egos.

When I joined as a masters degree student in the Education program at Azim Premji University, Bangalore, we had a maverick professor (in fact many of them!) named Dr. Kaustav Roy. Will write about him in detail later. He can be a subject for two–three blogs! What Kaustav Roy would do is name his courses in such a way that the academic body in the university would approve the course. He would add just one or two texts written by R. D Laing or Martin Heidegger as necessary readings. But in the class, all the focus would be on Laing or Heidegger. So we ended up learning about Phenomenology, Hermeneutics and Psychology of R D Laing etc. One such text was Laing's *The Politics of Experience and the Bird of Paradise*. Scottish psychiatrist R. D. Laing was a maverick too. Some of his quotes are so deeply etched in my mind that I can recite them in deep sleep.

Coming back to Laing and his famous quote that said that a good man is aware of the bad in him and is able to demotivate and neutralise that part, while a bad man is not even aware of it. It is in demotivating and eliminating the bad, the good survives. He further elaborates in another quote, "The range of what we think and do is limited by what we fail to notice. And because we fail to notice that we fail to notice, there is little we can do to change; until we notice how failing to notice shapes our thoughts and deeds."

While the prescription comes from the scientific world ofLaing, medicine is only available with the likes of Buddha, the venerated one. By the way, we Zennists venerate Buddha not because he is God, but because he is one of the ultimate teachers that ever lived.

While all other religious paths suggest worship and meditation etc. as the way of salvation, Buddha just focuses on our everyday life on this earth. Moment to moment. He was conspicuously silent about our time before birth or after death. He was mostly concerned about how we lived on this earth between those two milestones. My limited readings suggest to me that he was not a lot into the metaphysics of it. Buddhist meditation practices in general focus on our mind and body. Vipassana, Zazen, Shikantaza, Kinhin etc. train us to "notice when we fail to notice."

Almost every one of us would have read the quote of Viktor Frankl—which became viral from Stephen Covey's book *The 7 Habits ofHighly Effective People.* "Between stimulus and response, there is a space.In that space lies our power and freedom to choose our response. In those responses lie our freedom and happiness.

Meditation is one of the ways, I know of, to create that space.

While, as usual, citizens across India are raging for the harshest punishment to that rapist and murderer of the Kolkata doctor, it is worthwhile to consider encouraging our children, dear ones and others in our circle to meditate. I am in no way suggesting to do away with the law and justice system. However, if meditation—of course, they may or may not choose to meditate—does not help them to create that space between their ears, harsh punishment could be an option.

But not trying the greatest gift this nation has given to mankind before that ultimate act, is an act of crime in itself. And we have to try it out, not just on the Sanjoy Roys of this world, but on the BrijBhushans, Asarams, Strauss-Kahns, many heroes of the Malayalam movie industry, teachers who are charged with rape and/ or molesting their students, corporate leaders who abuse/ill-treat their subordinates…the list is endless! Like Mu! It includes ManKind. WomanKind too.

Chapter 6

Toothache of the Mind

2 August 2024

A long time ago, in November 2006, my father Sankara was a patient at the Surgical ICU (SICU) ward of Fortis Hospital, Bannerghatta Road—then Wockhardt Hospital—for four days. The SICU houses patients who have just undergone surgery. Some come back to life after stays in the ICU and a normal ward, then back home and their life. And some decide to end their suffering at the SICU. My father chose the second option. There were around 12–14 beds in that SICU and my father's bed was in a corner of that big hall. It was a short walk from the entrance to the bed. The notice board outside displayed the names and age of the patients and the doctor who had led the surgery. There was an infant too at that time. I don't remember her name but she was just three months old. Both she and my father were under the care of a famous cardiac surgeon.

During one of my conversations with the doctor, I asked him about the baby girl and the difficulties of operating on a tiny tot. His reply surprised me and I haven't forgotten his response.

He said, "On the contrary, babies cry only when they have real physical pain or are in need of something essential for their survival. Like when they are hungry or thirsty or they are in some physical discomfort. It can be taken care of quite easily. Only when we grow up and become adults do we cry over everything. Real or imaginary. Physical or mental. And then it becomes difficult."

At that time, I understood his words to some extent. Now, after some 18 years of living, not living, trying to read a bit of philosophy, Buddhism and practicing Zen, it was interesting to reflect on what he said.

His words sound so wise now.

Buddha's first teaching at Sarnath. The Four Noble Truths have the word suffering in all of them. As per his followers, Buddha is said to have said the word, dukkha. Though many translate the word dukkha as suffering, I would reckon, dissatisfaction is a closer translation. The Pali word dukkha, usually translated as suffering, has a more subtle range of meanings. Oriental traditions and thoughts are much more nuanced than the Occidental ones. Many times, much is lost in translation. Dukkha is also sometimes described metaphorically as a wheel that is off its axle.

It is important to keep in mind that traditional and conservative Buddhists ascribe everything in the *Tripitaka* to Buddha himself but many Buddhist scholars have identified many inconsistencies in those teachings. As in anything in life, the generations who passed it to their descendants would have done some value addition to them.

Zen Master AMA always reminds us to treat them critically. And I for one, as a Zen student, only swear by the *Kālāma Sutra*. Maybe that is how a rebellious and questioning mind reached the gateless gate of Zen, AMA Samy and Bodhi Sangha. Just a few months ago, noticing my overzealousness in devouring books on Zen and philosophy, AMA said, "One should not be too attached even to Zen and realisation. That too would be un-Zen-like." It's possible people like Nagarjuna lived that way and the result was Mahayana Buddhism and Zen. When the camel of Buddhism was made to pass through the needle hole of one of the greatest rationalist minds that ever lived, the result was *Madhyamika Karika*. It is not for nothing that someone like Jan WesterHoff, a noted authority on the religious traditions of the Orient, named Nagarjuna as one of the greatest philosophers and rationalists. While Mahayana Buddhists call him the Second Buddha, for Zennists, he is the first one.

Coming back to the toothache of the mind, there are three types of dukkha as per Buddhist teaching. Dukkha-dukkha, which means the suffering of suffering; Viparinama dukkha: the suffering of change; and Sankhara dukkha: the suffering of existence.

Toothache of the mind belongs to the first category, the suffering of suffering. The real toothache that afflicts one's body is curable and may disappear as the wheel of life rolls on. But it is difficult to cure the toothache of the mind. Have you ever observed patients waiting for their turn at a dentist's clinic? One suffers a lot more than necessary when one does not know how to suffer. It is our mind which transforms a probable fleeting pain of a moment in the future to an eternal one in our mind.

It is no different in other avenues of our life. When we were engineering students, we suffered while looking for a job. And when we landed a good job, we suffered once again because of the long work hours, a demanding boss or client, or even due to a colleague who managed to negotiate a better pay packet than we did or who received restricted stock units. We suffer when we don't have a car. And when we have one, we again suffer, while thinking about the possible traffic jams at Hebbal flyover or Silk Board junction.

Learning to Suffer

While Buddha's noble eightfold path talks about the end of suffering and the path to Nibbana, I tend to think, some suffering of existence (Sankhara dukkha) is needed to keep us ordinary humans real and alive. As Thich Nhat Hanh said, "If we learn to suffer well, we suffer less from suffering."

How do we learn to suffer? How do we build those mental muscles and develop mental resilience? The stoic way is one of the ways. But I find it very dry and robot-like. They teach you to anticipate what is going to happen and prepare you for it. Like a dose of vaccination.

In my humble view, the Orientalist practices are better and more effective.

First, Accept Reality as it is

Accepting reality as it is or seeing the world with a clear mind. Realising that life is what happens to you when you have other plans. When one gets Tinnitus (like me!) and learns that there is NO cure for it, one suffers only when one refuses to accept that fact of life. A few years ago, I found myself in deep depression due to Tinnitus. True, everything and everyone—friends, motivational talks, psychiatrist, medicines—helped me to an extent but what really helped me was meditation.

My psychiatrist, when I met him for the first time, did not rush to prescribe medicines. He said no one can withstand perfect silence. The maximum time one can stay in an anechoic chamber (the quietest place in the world) is just a few minutes. Let me quote from an article I found at the Smithsonian, and which I treasure in Evernote library, "Everybody seems to be looking for a little peace and quiet these days. But even such a reasonable idea can go too far. The quietest place on earth, an anechoic chamber at Or field Laboratories in Minnesota, is so eerily noiseless that visitors have used it to see how long they can stand the sound of their own bodies. It's completely silent inside the room—so silent that the background noise is measured in negative decibels, meaning it's below the threshold of human hearing. With no audible background noise to cover it up, visitors report hearing the sound of blood pumping in their heads or moving through their veins, according to Caity Weaver of the New York Times Magazine. Or, as Casey Darnell writes for the Star Tribune, you can even hear the sound of your eyelids shutting when you blink.

For those who have done Vipassana, one starts feeling the sensations in one's body. One starts hearing the voice of your cells on the 7th or 8th day as one goes deeper into oneself. So we are in a sense oriented towards it. But not for an anechoic chamber.

When you meditate on tinnitus, you realise that it is not one flat ghost noise in your mind. There are finer nuances to it. It changes tunes and rhythms. And it almost becomes musical. You realise that tinnitus is not different from you. You are tinnitus. Once you arrive at that realisation, tinnitus recedes to a far corner in the vast galaxy of your brain. And when you start meditating on tinnitus, instead of fighting it and yearning for no sound every moment of your waking life, the aha moment comes. Silence of the mind is different from the absence of sound. Even at the top of the Himalayas, one can get troubled by the silence while right in the midst of a noisy Silk Board flyover traffic jam, one can be at peace with oneself.

Accepting life as it happens to you at any moment is the first lesson on how to suffer and master suffering.

There is a famous saying,

"What your resist, persists."

– Undefined

It is important to understand that acceptance does not mean blind acceptance of learned helplessness. No way. It is just being aware of life as it unfolds, seeing reality as it is. We need to remember that every border that we draw between our experiences and us are also possible battle lines as well. It is in that choice-less awareness that your suffering gets extinguished.

Second, Live a Life of Gratitude

It is about being thankful for a state of no-toothache, once you are done with your toothache. When we are in the middle of a toothache or migraine, all we want is a state of no-toothache or no-migraine. But do we ever say to ourselves, what a nice day / moment?

No toothaches! It is not just some heartwarming chicken soup for the soul stuff! In an article in the *Scientific American*, Scott Barry Kauffman noted after conducting a study, that gratitude is the most predictive factor of one's well being. Love of learning comes second. Every other trait / character strength is a distant third to last.

I read that article almost three years after I started my daily journal on "Three Good Things in my Life". Thanks to Dr. Martin Seligman. And it did turn around my life. That is a story for another time!

So counting our blessings, seeing silver linings behind dark clouds, being happy with a plate of idli-vada or a hot cup of South Indian filter coffee, feeling uplifted by a smile from a loved one, an affectionate bark from Jackie Mu, an act of kindness and compassion from a stranger, the list of all the things that can be counted as the three blessings of a day, is endless.

It is so simple and straightforward. But when we feel gratitude for non-toothaches and no-migraines, it kind of lessens our suffering when suffering of Sankhara knocks on the doors of our mind.

Chapter 7

Man, Machine and the Search for Meaning

22 November 2011

My first meeting with Mr. Pai, about six years ago, lasted for an hour or so. I did meet him briefly again during an event at IIM Bangalore, but it was the initial meeting that left a lasting impression on me. Don't get me wrong; I am not a star-struck, name-dropping fanboy looking for my five minutes of fame. In fact, many of his past and present colleagues would agree that an invite to meet with the reigning—now dethroned—Tsar was not something that anyone looked forward to.

Despite the many colourful and captivating stories about his notorious temper, I felt no apprehension, perhaps because of the communist DNA in me, as I walked through the pristine corridors to meet him and his team. Fun fact: this company probably ensures the success of Reckitt Benckiser or P&G in India. A naïve visitor may even wonder if they have OCD like Lady Macbeth!

Mr. Pai's physical presence is quite imposing, even with that half-friendly smile. Built like a wrestler, his unkempt beard and baritone voice added to the total effect. Contrary to expectations, he came across as an honest and straightforward man who practices what he preaches. Unlike many others who remain paper idealists. I sensed that the mandate of "taking care of his organisation" took precedence over his own views and values. I remember it wasn't easy to verbally spar with someone with such razor sharp intelligence and crystal-clear articulation. True, there were traces of ruthlessness, like Gary

Kasparov playing mind games with Viswanathan Anand, but then he showed signs of compassion and fairness especially when sharing his experiences and how they had shaped his own career.

Many who worked in that company told me that he was quite instrumental in the success of that iconic organisation. He was always seen as a future CEO. His own success stories, his financial wizardry as CFO—hailing as he did from South Canara—and his stint as a director with a huge span of responsibility added to that myth. So it surprised many when he resigned.

But what really struck me were his statements in those endless interviews after the announcement. He said, "I feel liberated", "I feel free," and "Life is all about tomorrow. You know I am a Bangalore guy but I have not had lunch at a restaurant in the city in the past 17 years. I want to spend a lot of time with my wife, kids and friends. I want to catch up on my reading. My wife has bought me a houseful of books. Also, I want to destress and tame my temper."

It left one wondering: was he truly enjoying his stint? Or was it just an adrenaline pumping, teeth gritting kind of forced motivation born out of ambition to prove a point? It also raises an important question: while accepting that earning a living, contributing to society and the organisation, leaving a legacy etc are all worthy pursuits, does it have to be at the cost of everything else?

Charlie Chaplin in Modern Times movie. Pic courtesy: https://photo. charliechaplin.com/images/1617-mt-149-jpg

Does Life have to be a Single Spoked Wheel?

Is it a wrong notion in our circles that life has to be single dimensional?

Did Gandhi not take time out to listen to an M.S. Subbulakshmi keerthan, even when he was racing against time to achieve India's independence? How many know that Einstein was a gifted violinist and Richard Feynman learned to paint and play drums? Ratan Tata enjoyed flying planes and sketching. And Jack Welch truly worried about his golf scores and diligently worked on them. Were/Are their contributions to society and their chosen fields any less when compared to that of others?

There is an interesting story about one of the most successful generals of the Indian Army. So innovative was his operational planning and so meticulous its execution that Lt-Gen J.S. Aurora did not forsake his daily round of golf even once during the 12-day battle to "liberate" East Pakistan, which emerged as Bangladesh in 1971. As India's Eastern Army commander tasked with evicting the tyrannical Pakistani military from East Pakistan, the Sikh soldier even played a relaxed 18-hole round inside his Fort William headquarters at Calcutta, before leaving for Dacca to accept the surrender of Lt-Gen A.A.K. Niazi and 93,000 soldiers.

These are all pointers to the fact that there are many great souls who excelled in their chosen field without depriving themselves of the good moments of life. A common denominator in all of them was a multi dimensional approach to life. A single-minded focus on the goal, be it achieving enlightenment, becoming a prime minister or a CEO, does not mean being oblivious to all other fine aspects of this wonderful life. Considering a finished painting as a metaphor for one's life, if one stops insisting on being the sole creator of the painting and lets life paint a few brushstrokes, then we may have a masterpiece. That happens only when one accepts the truth that life is what happens to you here and now.

Life is not necessarily what happens tomorrow.Because tomorrow never comes.

Endnote: This non-aspiring Taoist non-writer earns his living working for the IT industry.

The Way I See that is absolutely his personal perception (or lack of IT) and relatively nothing official about IT.

Chapter 8

Language in Thoughtless Inaction

Ever since I attended a month-long NLP course under the venerable guidance of the NLP Guru, Jesuit Priest and Indo-American Dr. Richard McHugh—who, in my opinion, is more Indian than many born and raised here— I have been fascinated by language constructs.

Dr. Richard McHugh, S.J>

My good friend and trainer, Daniel Pacheco, who studied NLP under the maverick Richard Bandler, often says that anything people say has three meanings: stated, understood and hidden. And I would hasten to add that most often, we miss all three.

S.I. Hayakawa's classic book, *Language in Thought and Action*, reinforced this belief. Written some 70 years ago, this small but profound book offers invaluable insights into how language affects human thought and conditions behaviour, and how it should be used to foster cooperation and understanding, rather than conflict and confrontation.

Recently, the Time magazine published an intriguing article about two well-meaning ladies in Mexico. The report stated, "The survival of an endangered language may depend on two people but all they want to do is ignore each other. Manuel Segovia and Isidro Velazquez, the last speakers of the Ayapaneco language, live less than half a mile away from each other in Ayapa, Mexico. But no matter how precious the cultural implications of keeping their language alive are, they are not going to speak to each other."

The Guardian added, "It is not clear whether there is along-buried argument behind their mutual avoidance, but people who know them say they have never really enjoyed each other's company."

Sadly, Ayapaneco is one of many indigenous languages in Mexico teetering on the brink of extinction. Linguists are valiantly trying to preserve the language despite the lack of communication between the last two fluent speakers. Segovia, 75, and Velazquez, 65, no longer converse regularly in their native tongue. When they pass away, their language will die with them. Linguistic anthropologist Daniel Suslak sums up their relationship succinctly, "They don't have a lot in common."

Language Shapes Our Thoughts and Actions

Senator Hayakawa emphasises the importance of how we use a language. After all, language shapes our thoughts and exerts extraordinary influence on ourselves and others.

What happens when we cease to use a language? Do we stop thinking? How do we influence others?

It is said that, "By age four, most humans have developed the ability to communicate through oral language. By age six or seven, most can comprehend and express written thoughts. These unique abilities of communicating through a native language clearly separate humans from all animals."

The animal closest to producing human-like speech is not another primate, but a bird. For instance, a famous African gray parrot in England named Toto can pronounce words so clearly that he sounds almost human. Like humans, birds can produce fluent, complex sounds. I remember, during my childhood, my cousin had a myna that could utter a few words.

One of the success stories of exploring human-like qualities in non-human primates is Kanzi, a male bonobo chimpanzee born on October 28, 1980. Kanzi's journey to learn to "speak" began through training given to his mother, Matata, via a "talking" keyboard. Matata never mastered it but Kanzi did. Through years of intense training and close social contact with humans, Kanzi achieved the language abilities of an average two-year-old human. By age ten, he had a vocabulary (via the keyboard) of some 200 words. In fact, Kanzi was able to go beyond the mere parroting or "aping"of humans; he could actually communicate his feelings, needs, and even use tools.

In one instance, during an outing in the Georgia woods, Kanzi touched the symbols for marshmallows and fire. Given matches and marshmallows, Kanzi snapped twigs for a fire, lit them with the matches, and toasted the marshmallows on a stick.

The tragedy is that while such animals make sincere attempts to master language, the single most differentiating factor between animals and humans is that we humans often cease to communicate.

Chapter 9

Practice of Best Practices: Is it Always the Case of "Could have been Better?"

15 March 2012

I don't quite recall when I first read it—perhaps six or seven years ago—but I clearly remember where: in the pages of *The Hindu*. What stuck with me was the phrase:

"That was Best, could have been better."

– Nirmal Shekhar

That interesting article, penned by the brilliant wordsmith Nirmal Shekar, still lingers in my memory. Maybe the gene I inherited has a soccer chromosome. Or is it the wonderful and enviable prose that Shekar strings together like poetry about sports? It was an obituary for George Best, the football legend—a tribute both well-deserved and beautifully crafted.

George Best in 1976. Photo courtesy: Wikipedia

This memory resurfaced from the depths of my rather greying web of neurons during a recent conversation with a friend about what else, but the "Practice of best practices." I found myself explaining, with some effort, that what works wonders in one context may flop magnificently at another.

Nature gets it, unfortunately we often don't.The giant redwood sequoia trees thrive in California, but in the arid sand dunes of Arabia, the hardy cactus is more viable. Yet, in the corporate world, the term "best practice" is thrown around with reckless abandon, as if it's a universal remedy for all ills.

Though this hackneyed phrase about best practice has been done to death in the corporate world, I think our tendency to latch onto best practices might be rooted in our evolutionary history. I'd venture to say that the practice of best practices and the survival of mankind have evolved hand in hand. My conviction springs from my reflections on Aswath Damodaran's insights on risk. In my opinion, his book *Strategic Risk Taking: A Framework for Risk Management* is the best book on risk. The average lifespan of our ancestors was less than 40. They lived short and unforgiving lives. Their decisions, often made in the blink of an eye, were driven by the reptilian brain. The moments of truth such as, *"Get your supper or be one,"* never affords one the luxury of strategic deliberation—there was always one best way to evade a predator.

Remember the comedy *The Gods Must be Crazy?* In it, an African bushman travels to the end of the earth to get rid of a troublesome Coca-Cola bottle. A memorable scene is the one with the little boy and the menacing hyena. The way the young boy tried to appear bigger than the hyena is a classic best practice. I would recommend one of my favourite books, *Cry of the Kalahari*, in which Mark and Delia Owens documented their own experiences with the lions of Kalahari. It is said, "If you see a lion, do not try to run away or turn your back on the animal. Try to make and hold eye-contact with the lion. With many cat species, prolonged eye-contact is a sign of dominance. Try to appear larger, in any way possible. If you have a child with you, try to put them on your shoulders, to make you appear even bigger."

Moving forward, lions have given way to modern buildings. Almost all best practices have originated from four human endeavours: construction, farming, shipping and war. For instance, ancient Romans followed a quirky method of ensuring quality. When the scaffolding of the grand arches was removed, the builder had to stand beneath the arch—a strong incentive for a good job indeed. Some of those arches still stand today. The ones that did not were the ones under which the architect was buried alive, half dead or dead. I really wish one of my good friends, who makes millions from the clinical research of medicines, would adopt this practice.

The point being made is that our ancestors always had just one way to survive. Either learn about the wisdom of the way from the "One fortunate one" who survived to tell his story, or perish. The choice was that simple. This ingrained the concept of best practice into our subconscious, like the fight-or-flight response.

Times have changed but acquired habits have not.

While the corporate jungle is no different thematically, we're fortunate that we don't have to rely only on instinct, but can apply thought. As consultants, it is important for us to shed the mantra of "What's good for Peter is good for Paul."

One best practice that will always stand is to **ADAPT**—to the new factors—culture, environment, constraints and possibilities. Become **ADEPT** before **ADOPT**ing a practice. Or we may end up hearing the same refrain, **"That was BEST, but it could have been better."**

Chapter 10

Lasting Impressions of Some Remarkable Lives from Close Quarters

12 July 2009

As our bus rolled into Mannarkkad, across the new bridge over Nellipuzha River, I felt a strong connection to the land I was born in, raised and had lived in for many years. My brother Sasi and I were here to help our mother pack up and leave for Kollegal, her home before marriage. It was a sad day, just about 24 hours had passed since the funeral of Raja mama in Mysore, a true son of the soil

Our neighbour at Mannarkkad, a "well meaning" lady, said it was really sad that my mother, who had lived at Mannarkkad for over 40 years, had to leave. In her view it was sadder than Raja mama's death. My mind failed to understand her logic. I also failed to convince her that it hardly matters, since all of us would have to leave one day, sooner or later.

I had mentally left Mannarkkad the moment my dear dad was buried in what is probably the most scenic burial ground in the world, nestled beside the river he loved so much. When a local strongman tried to take over the land owned by the small and dwindling Kannada-speaking community, where generations of our ancestors lay silently listening to the hoary tunes of the Kunthipuzha river, my father fought fiercely to keep the place in our hands.

He ensured that no greedy land grabber would encroach and disturb his last slumber.

After having faced so many tragic moments lately, it seemed strange that this loss felt so different. I couldn't quite put my finger on it. Maybe it's only when someone close goes back to Mother Earth that we steal a few precious moments to step back and think about what life means to us and more importantly, what matters to us. Then it struck me that it was the people who still live in my mind long after they are gone, they matter. It had nothing to do with the environment.

There haven't been too many such souls in my life. I could probably count the names on my fingers. They weren't famous, they were just remarkable people who lived remarkable lives and left an indelible mark on me. When they passed, only their loved ones mourned and prayed for them. I have known some of them closely for many years, while I have spent only a few hours with the others. Yet, their impact on me has been profound.

This is my homage to them. I am not sure whether all the impressions I carry in my mind were captured through my own eyes during my time with them or shaped by the legends I've heard about them. It doesn't really matter. It should not, for you as well. Nothing is more malleable than reality. Life itself becomes the ultimate creative act, as you realise and become aware that you shape your world through your thoughts.

Let me start with the one whose untimely demise triggered these thoughts.

Infinite Grace: The Life of Raja Mama

Infinite grace—that is how Raja mama lived and left this world. If grace is infinite, how could anyone be outside its boundaries? He treated everyone with equal warmth, whether it was the mentally challenged, but physically fit, son of the neighbourhood tea stall owner or one of his wealthy friends, some of whom had inherited thousands of acres of land. His door was always open.

His contagious and ready smile accompanied by an affectionate greeting always welcomed us.

I always saw him poised and composed, never hurried or harried. He effortlessly put people at ease. He was always dressed elegantly. Even during his final months, when he was confined to a wheelchair, nobody would have found him looking unkempt or in shabby clothes.

It was remarkable how Raja mama faced his terminal illness. He fought a valiant battle against the crippling illness with infinite grace. Maybe he had decided, even when he had insufferable pains, he did not have to be limited by his discomfort. He was someone who organised a surprise birthday party for his wife from his wheelchair, looked after my aged uncle who did not have many in his own family to look after him, and even tried to find a suitable bridegroom for my sister-in-law.

He was a mentor par excellence for many in my generation and played a pivotal role in my life. He convinced me to stay back and complete my engineering degree in Hubli, and later helped me find my life partner too. I remember him teaching me that enjoying an evening drink is not a sin as long as I know my limits! And more importantly, he showed us a fine and gracious way of living in the present, for the future.

Two incidents spring to my mind. First, even while waiting for an appointment for bypass surgery at Narayana Hrudayalaya, he quizzed and guided my brother about getting air-conditioning for the restaurant my brother was planning to start at Mysore; second, the way he was looking forward to play card games from his wheelchair. For him the present is what really mattered and the past was left way behind where it belonged. His positivity, generosity, kindness and spirit will live on, far beyond his passing.

The Brilliant Mind: Neelakanta Doddappa

Neelakanta Doddappa, my father's first cousin and one of his closest friends, was a man of extraordinary intellect. He was someone who could challenge World Bank consultants from Canada on the design of the arch dam at Idukki; he also brought in innovative changes in hydroelectric dam designs and that earned him an honorary membership at the American Society of Civil Engineers. The story goes that one of the consultants forwarded his brilliant ideas and that was enough to earn him an honorary membership. If he had not been afflicted with Parkinson's disease at a pretty early age, I think he would have made quite an impact in India like an E.M. Sreedharan.

When I joined engineering college, he gifted me an old book on metrics and measurement—originally written in German—saying it was all I needed to know as an engineer, besides the basic principles. He once told my dad that he found it difficult to remember many things including faces, but what he never forgets was mathematics. It was quite amazing to see him solve problems in integral calculus; during those moments it seemed like his mind was free from the clutches of the disease. Last month, I met his intermediate classmate, my high school headmaster, who remarked that if anyone could answer all the questions in a modern day engineering entrance exam, it would be Neelakantan. Probably that compliment from a class mate after 60 odd years says it all.

Though I lost the book he gave me, I kept something far more valuable—his signature. I modelled my own signature after his, though his was more precise, like the arch dam he so masterfully designed.

The Stoic Scholar: Gopalathatha

Gopalathatha, my grandmother's cousin and my favourite teacher, introduced me to the world of Jiddu Krishnamurti, Fritjof Capra and rationalism. I first saw Gopalathatha when he walked in to attend his estranged brother's funeral. I had learned about his long absence from home after some misunderstanding years ago. Upon his return, the first thing he did was to open a free tuition center. And soon my Dad ushered my brother and me into his class. I continued there for a very long time, right until his death.

He was a remarkable human being and teacher who was one of the early recipients of the National Teacher Award. He was a man of immense knowledge, particularly in English Literature, Philosophy and Economics. Despite the tragedies in his life—the early loss of his wife and later, his son's death from leukemia—he remained focused on his mission to impart knowledge.

For some reason, he relegated his photo with Ms. Indira Gandhi to the corner of an inner room (maybe after the Emergency), but behind his desk, he proudly displayed the brass peacock, along with a note, from one of his students. He was someone who led his life like a disciplined Zen master, with pristine purity; very much like his usual attire of a white shirt and dhoti.

What stayed with me was his stoic demeanour, even at his son's funeral, and his ability to convey deep meaning through short, simple sentences. To me it seemed like he maintained a clinical distance from his emotions and pain, living like a disciplined Zen master.

My last memory is him on his hospital bed. He had been diagnosed with cancer, which had spread throughout his body. I had taken the small book of *Siddhartha* to read during my one-hour long trip from Mannarkkad to the hospital in Perinthalmanna. He asked me to read a passage from it and as I was reading the passage about rebirth he stopped me. He told me about how Albert Camus, one of his favourite authors, died in a road accident despite hating road travel. In fact, Camus had a train ticket in his pocket when he died. Gopalathatha passed away within another week and I decided not to attend his funeral. I wanted to retain my last memory of him as it is.

The ever-present spirit of my father

Lastly, I wanted to write about my dad, but then I don't think he has ever gone away from me. He was the kindest and most generous soul I have ever known and was always there for me and I am sure he will always be.

I'm not sure if they read blogs in heaven, or if heaven even exists. But wherever these souls are, I wish them well with all my heart and immense gratitude.

Chapter 11

Oh! Are You People Going to Talk About Things You Don't Know Much About?

15 September 2024

Around 10 years ago, on a Sunday morning—Manu was probably in middle school at The Valley School during those years—I was getting ready to go to the school for the monthly study meet on Krishnamurti's teachings. Ever since we moved into Kanakapura Road, going to this meet had become a kind of ritual for me. Many Krishnamurti-ites gathered every first Sunday of each month at The Valley School, KFI. We formed smaller groups and discussed a topic. We watched a K-talk video and then had a spartan lunch at the school mess.

When I was a high school student at Mannarkkad, I used to go to my father's uncle for tuition. We called him Gopalathatha. He was a national award-winning teacher, very well read and erudite with a huge collection of books. As someone who had graduated from then-Madras, he had a keen interest in Krishnamurti's teachings. Gopalathatha told me once that he used to go to Vasant Vihar to listen to K and along with a few books, he also had a couple of audio tapes of his talks. Though I did try to read a bit, I soon gave it up as the philosophy was a bit heavy for me at that time.

K returned to my life when Thara's grand uncle visited us in Bangalore. He had been one of the earliest students of Rishi Valley School and he instructed Thara and me to consider K schools for our children. That is why we shifted to Mantri Tranquil on Kanakapura Road, to be closer to The Valley School campus. During my first visit to the study center, I fell in love with their library. They had a vast collection of books on philosophy and K. I felt like a child in a candy shop. Soon I found myself in the worlds of the Krishnamurtis (Jiddu and UG). While I read and reread all the major books of K, I used to go and meet UG whenever he came to Padmanabhanagar, Bangalore.

The K. Krishnamurtis: Jiddu and UG.

(Once UG asked me to get out when I persistently defended Jiddu Krishnamurti.)

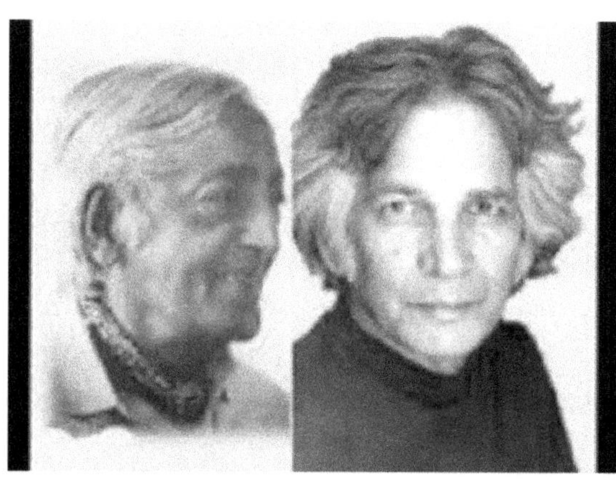

Every Thursday we had similar study groups at the K Study Center in the school campus and every month, we attended a three-day long retreat too. And once every year, there is an annual KFI gathering in one of the K Schools. It gradually extended to our PTM meetings too, along with the children and the teachers. During those times, I was an active participant in all the discussions and dialogues. I participated for two reasons. It gave me an opportunity to test my understanding, like a touchstone, and secondly there were brilliant minds amongst them.

Two of them kind of took me under their wings. Dr. Satish Inamdar, who left a career as a cancer surgeon, was the school director and a KFI trustee, and Prof Krishna Nath, who was are retired professor from Kashi Mahavidyalaya, and a close associate of Ram Manohar Lohia and Achyut Patwardhan. He was a scholar on both Vedas and Buddhism, and he organised the dialogue between Buddhist scholars and Krishnamurti atVaranasi. He was very close to the Dalai Lama too.

Prof Krishnanath

Dr Satish Imandar

Over the years, although I have met Dr. Harshad Parekh, Kabir Jaithirtha, Swami Chidananda, Mark Lee, AlokMathur, Dr. Shailesh Shirali etc. the meetings have not been very significant. Shri V.D. Kulkarni, who was my good friend Deepak's father, used to stay for long stretches at the study center campus and recommended books to me. Dr. Gajanan Rao, who is a trustee of KFI and runs a hospital in Chennai, asked me to translate K's thoughts into Malayalam and put me in touch with editor Krishnamurti at Vasanta Vihar. They were not only brilliant but quite compassionate too. They frequently tolerated non-aligned views and arguments for the sake of argument from a spiritual upstart like me. And I really looked forward to those long conversations with them.

Coming back to my Sunday morning, as I was getting ready to leave, Manu appeared from nowhere and asked the question that hit me like a thunderbolt!

"Oh! Are you people going to talk about things you don't know!"

It was probably the matter-of-fact way in which he asked the question that it hit me very hard. Right between my eyes. Instead of going for the study meet, I ended up sitting at my desk and began reflecting on the impact of Manu's arrow. That is when I understood Dr. Inamdar and Prof Krishna Nath's constant urging to stop reading and instead, live K's teachings.

I stopped going to the philosophical dialogues altogether. That helped me distance myself from K's teaching. Guess, when I was in the middle of it, I had missed his core message. Though I did attend a few more study meets, they were all part of parent-teacher meetings for Manu and Rishi.

A few years later, as a student of Education at Azim Premji University, I signed up for Phenomenology and Epistemology. Phenomenology was taught by Dr. Kaustav Roy and Epistemology by Dr. Indrani Bhattacharji. Kaustav Roy, a real maverick in principle and practice, was a star at the university and his classes were always overflowing. I made it a point to sit in his classes for all four semesters. And for the final semester, he was my guide for my thesis work, Phenomenological Study of Krishnamurti's Teachings.

Dr. Indrani was no less of a maverick. When her CV states,"Dr. Indrani Bhattacharjee has doctoral degrees in philosophy from Jadavpur University and the University of Massachusetts, Amherst," you know it.

Phenomenology and Epistemology are two ends of the spectrum in philosophy. It was my habit in Epistemology class to always raise a doubt with Prof. Roy. And he would clinically destroy my argument. Once, the moment he started his class, I asked a question on Descartes' Cogito Ergo Sum, and the rest of the class was a classic critique of where Descartes went wrong and how it had kind of messed up the Western civilisation.

Those years as a student of education taught me the limitations of knowledge. More knowledge does not necessarily mean freedom of the human mind. Rather, it enslaves us more and more to concepts and theories.

About a year and a half ago, as part of the admission process to one of the premier university in India. Manu had to write an essay on why capitalism is better than communism. In his usual rebellious way, he chose to write why committing one's mind to one "ism" limits our ability to evaluate another. When I turned down their offer of admission to him due to the high fees, an asst prof who was part of their admission office called me and told me that they were ready to give Manu a scholarship and they were thrilled to read his essays.

Manu knew instinctively what I had missed altogether.

Younger versions of Manu and Rishi after they pushed me out of the meditation mat. While Manu lectured me on the importance of play instead of meditation, Rishi's face says it all. Why don't elders ever get it?

As K rightly said, the root of human problems and suffering is the fact that we take creation of our thoughts as real and sacrosanct.

However, the truth is that our knowledge and concepts limit our ability to know reality as it is. When Fr. AMA Samy keeps reminding me that Zen is beyond concepts and theories, it is no different from what K taught. And Lao Tu knew it better than anyone else when he said: **Those who know** do not **speak. Those who speak** do not **know.**

Chapter 12

Zen and the Fine Art of Dishwashing

31 August 2024

Here's a long list of ideas and thoughts that I'm hopping around with, like a butterfly in the garden of ideas!

Brother Thay preparing his meal. Photo courtesy: Plum Village Web site

It was a chilly yet pleasant Tuesday evening at the Little Flower Zendo, Perumalmalai. Most evenings here are pleasant—the mornings, days and nights too! The sky was covered with dark rain clouds and thick blankets of fog enveloped everything else. Fog in the blue mountains can blind any one including advanced manmade machines. The tragic chopper accident that killed many, including our ex-Defence Chief, happened during the day near Ooty.

And to add to the atmosphere, it was pitch dark. One could say carbon-black dark. It was time to sleep for all sentient beings but the sounds of crickets and the roar of the Little Flower Zendo waterfall made a bad symphony. The recent rains seems to have helped the waterfall to regain her mojo and the reclaiming roar overwhelmed all other sounds of nature. Whenever I look at that waterfall—since it is just across my window , which is where I spend most of my waking or working time—what comes to mind is the immortal punch line of Bruce Lee about water. "Empty your mind, be formless, shapeless, like water."

Zen Master Fr. AMA Samy was just back at the Zendo from his month-long European tour, where he led Zen Sesshins in Germany, Sweden and Vienna. He is 89 years young. He had a stopover at Dubai, a long wait in Chennai airport followed by a long drive from Madurai to Kodaikanal. Road repair works made the drive even longer than the usual 3–3.5 hrs. He joined us for tea and said he was quite exhausted. He asked me about the Kōan I was working on. I was at Mumonkan 12: Zuigan calls his Master. Assuming that he would be tired, in typical management consultant style, I suggested that we could conduct the Dokusan the next day. AMA smiled at me compassionately and retired to his room. I too happily signed off for the day.

From Ontology...

Since Jio's internet signals were still going strong, I logged into the teaser(marketing) session of Ontology in Leadership Coaching. I was looking forward to it. I did have a 1-minute elevator pitch knowledge of Ontology, but then I am a 1-minute expert on almost all the things under the sun including Zen, which means I can deliver a punchy opening line for a minute and then move on to the next topic. Although I had taken courses in Phenomenology, Hermeneutics andEpistemology at Azim Premji University, I had not studied Ontology at all. As the facilitator held up the card with O—> A-> R written in bold—meaning the way of being precedes action and result—there was a LinkedIn alert on my screen about an article Jayanth had posted.

Jayanth was an ex-senior colleague in the Business Change Management practice at WiproConsulting and had done well for himself in that area. He is now a partner forCulture and Change with a leading consulting firm. He is quite a thought leader in that area. I thought I would glance at the article and get back to the session. The article was written by his CEO. The opening lines were rather interesting and I chose to read the article. That is what triggered writing this blog. And that's how life is. Life is what happens to you when you plan for other things.

To Finding Meaning in Work

The summary of the article read, "In today's work culture, transforming mandatory tasks into fulfilling activities is crucial for motivation. This article explores how shifting from 'have to' to 'want to' can enhance job satisfaction and productivity. Discover strategies to make this shift and share these insights with your network." The marketing byline of the solution from the article was, "How leaders can help find meaning—and sometimes excitement—in their work."

What came to my mind as a flash was a very old interview of K.V. Kamath in Rediff. For the uninitiated, K.V. Kamath was a legendary banker and corporate leader who succeeded another (more ?) legendary banker and corporate leader N Vaghul atICICI. Rediff was the only website that many of us, netizens of my generation, accessed until quite recent times. The interview was dated 09 Feb 2005 and Mr. Kamath talked about motivation, or lack thereof, amongst the brightest Indian talent he had recruited from then leading Indian B Schools. Let me quote from the article.

It is worth reading.

KV Kamath: ICICI had a problem of atrophy, and we had to break out of it if we were to survive. In 1996–1997, we had this wonderful situation where youngsters would come and atrophy within a year. They were a small group of 20, all from the top 10 per cent of the four major B-schools. One day I asked one of these youngsters to mail merge 25 letters. Two days later I asked what happened to those letters. He made some excuses. I went back to my room and in 20 minutes Idid the mail merge, printed out the letters, signed them, and left them on his table.

My colleague, Executive Director Nachiket Mor, threw up his hands in frustration. His question was, "What has changed these youngsters?" They were bright and bubbly, top of the class people. Yet within six to eight months of working atICICI, they had atrophied, lost their motivation. The atrophy ran deep.

https://www.rediff.com/money/2005/feb/09bspec.htm

So what Jayanth's CEO was discussing was not a new problem. It was rather surprising.Regardless of the advancements we had made in our life, in technology, neuroscience, psychology etc. from 1996–2024, one of the management problems was still the same! And the moot point was how did Kamath help that "great talent" from a premier B School find meaning, leave alone find excitement, in a mundane task.

I won't be wrong if I stated that one of the most researched topics in management is"methods to boost employee motivation and productivity."

Two cliched ways I intend to avoid: one, I will not list down the reasons why we do, or don't do, what we do or don't do; second, I will not give a laundry list of 1, 2, 3… on how to quickly fix the problem. Ever since Stephen Covey wrote that classic book on personal transformation, it has become fashionable to list down a few solutions!

Also, I am not going to take the finding-purpose route. As I have understood from my own life, my purpose in life is not divinely ordained. Rather I am the one who defines/ projects meaning and purpose in my day-to-day life. That is because,God, nature, Mu, essence or emptiness is not a dictator, but s/he/it is the master change or transformation manager and knows very well that it is better to give that choice to us. Or why would all of us have been endowed with freewill or agency to decide what we want from this world, what we want to give to the world and what we want to become?

Even otherwise, just imagine, finding our purpose in cleaning a full basket of dirty dishes, or mopping the floor, cleaning up our cupboard, dusting our book shelf or as Kamath wrote, create a mail bulletin to share with customers ……..

As I learnt from AMA Samy, in Zen there is no why. From moment to moment, you are called upon by life and you respond to that call. You become yourself in this cycle of call and response.

Food for thought: Again, it is worthwhile asking, do we need to be inspired and stay pumped up all the time? Most people don't realize that depending on adrenaline and dopamine to motivate us takes us down a slippery slope. They work like psychedelic drugs.Our bodies easily build up tolerance to such chemicals and motivators, whether that is intrinsic to our body or mind, or external to us.

Be Present in Everything That We Do

The following day, as I was lighting the lamp at the Zendo in preparation for the morning Zazen at 5:30 am, AMA was there. I was going to lead the sesshin as Zendo leader and was in charge of bells and recitals. Zen bells are a bit complicated. We have different types of bells for different intents and a different way of holding them etc. As usual I made my quota of mistakes. And I was happy when I thought no one else noticed them. After breakfast, AMA called me into the Zendo again and asked me to sit on the meditation cushion. He satin front of me on the floor in Vajrasana and taught me how to do it properly.He did it so slowly and in such a measured way, and with so much patience and compassion, that for a moment I knew what Zen was. He said that in Zen nothing is more holy or less holy. And nothing is unholy. In our ordinary life, all ordinary moments are extraordinary and it is important to be present in anything we do. And that is Zen. Nothing more, nothing less.

All the while, I kept thinking about my blog on Zen and the fine art of dish washing. I wondered what really motivates a Zen master.

What Motivates an Ordinary Human?

So what motivates an ordinary human with an ordinary mind and ordinary life like mine?I found my answer when I was saving myself from deep depression and padding upto bat for the second innings of my life. Rather than digging through the skeletons of reasons that landed me in that terrible state, I would rather write about what got me out of that deep dark well.

It was almost a bootstrap process. In computers, a bootstrap program is the first line of code that runs and loads the operating system. The entire operating system depends on the bootstrap program working correctly. In my case, it was the compassion of my dear ones and my mentors that worked as a bootstrap code for me. More on that later.

My insight from the whole trauma is that we lose our mind when we get stuck between the heaviness of our past and the fear and concerns of the future. To paraphrase that immortal sentence of Viktor Frankl—made famous by Stephen Covey—

> *"Between past and the future, there is a small sliver of moment which we call present. In that moment, lies our freedom to be. And in that being lies our joy and peace. We lose our mind when our past meets the future, and the sliver of the moment disappears with our wellness and joy."*
>
> *– Vishy Sankara*

Jiddu Krishnamurti wrote, "Because time is fear and if the mind of a human being is to be totally free of fear psychologically, completely, absolutely to be free of fear, he must understand time. Time as the movement of thought. And is there an action which is without time? That is: time ends, action begins."

The moment we understand that fear is a product of our thought, and it does not have an independent existence from our thought, it dissolves into nothingness.He goes on to add the example of a mountain and a microphone. A mountain is not created by thought. It exists independent of thought. But a microphone—ora computer or an iPad —is created by our thoughts. It too exists independent of thought. Likewise, fear too is created by thought like the concept of "Me / I."But our mind tends to think that Fear, Me /I also exist independent of thought.All our misery and suffering start from this.

It is also interesting that we think about the present moment as the current second we are aware of. Krishnamurti spent a lifetime trying to teach his audience that psychological time is not the same as chronological time.

Have you read the wonderful poem

Time is by Henry Van Dyke? "Time is too slow for those who wait,

Too swift for those who fear,

Too long for those who grieve,

Too short for those who rejoice;

But for those who love,

Time is not."

As we stop living in the past and future, the space between them expands and our living in the present can stretch to an eon.

Let's talk about value, meaning the value we put on things, is also a creation of our thoughts. In the mid-19th century, Napoleon III served his most honoured guests' meals on aluminium plates, while the less privileged were forced to have their meals on gold or silver plates.

The value we assign to things is subjective and contextual. It is just a property we assign to a thing—a product, a service, a person, an experience. Nothing more. When Adam Smith and capitalism won over Marx and Marxism, it also affected our brain's ventral striatum[4] . As we progressed across generations, what is priced in the market space ended up becoming more valuable to us. The market does not reward the process or journey, and what you gain in the process of your personal journey is of little interest to the marketplace. So the focus is always on the destination or product. Again, we hardly realise the carrot dangling in front of the donkey is always in the future.

How Does All This Add Up in the Fine Art of Dishwashing?

We tend to pick and choose what we want to do or avoid, because our mind is preprogrammed in such a way that we have become slaves of our memories and future projections when it comes to value or misery.

When we become aware, we start living in the present. Anything that we do with awareness becomes a joyful activity. Samu (service) is not different from Zazen in Zen. Even making a cup of tea and serving it is of spiritual value. We don't realise it but even that simple act opens up our creative mind. And it is quite amazing that when our minds are still and empty of thoughts, it frees us from the heavy baggage of memory of the past and the fear and paranoia about an uncertain future.

Discarding the Baggage of Past Memories

Let me quote one of my favourite paras from Robert M. Pirsig's *Zen and the Art of Motorcycle Maintenance*. This is about an incident when Pirsig was teaching creative writing to university students at Montana.

Pirsig had been having trouble with students who had nothing to say. At first he thought it was laziness but later it became apparent that it wasn't. They just couldn't think of anything to say. One of them, a girl with quite powerful glasses, wanted to write a 500-word essay about the UnitedStates. He was used to the sinking feeling that comes from statements like this and suggested, without disparagement, that she narrow it down to just Bozeman.When the paper was due, she didn't have it and was quite upset. She had tried and tried but she just couldn't think of anything to say.

He had already discussed her with her previous instructors and they'd confirmed his impressions of her. She was very serious, disciplined and hardworking, but extremely dull. Not a spark of creativity in her anywhere. Here yes, behind the thick-lensed glasses, were the eyes of a drudge. She wasn't bluffing him, she really couldn't think of anything to say and was upset by her inability to do as she was told.

It just stumped him. Now *he* couldn't think of anything to say. A silence occurred, and then a peculiar answer: "Narrow it down to the main street of Bozeman." It was a stroke of insight. She nodded dutifully and went out. But just before her next class she came back in real distress, in tears this time, distress that had obviously been there for a long time. She still couldn't think of anything to say, and couldn't understand why, if she couldn't think of anything about all of Bozeman, she should be able to think of something about just one street.

He was furious. "You're not looking!" he said. A memory came back of his own dismissal from the university for having too much to say. For every fact there is an infinity of hypotheses. The more you look the more you see. She really wasn't looking and yet somehow didn't understand this.

He told her angrily, "Narrow it down to the front of one building on the main street of Bozeman. The Opera House. Start with the upper left-hand brick."

Her eyes, behind the thick-lensed glasses, opened wide. She came to the next class with a puzzled look and handed him a 5000-word essay on the front of the Opera House on the main street of Bozeman, Montana. "I sat in the hamburger stand across the street," she said, "and started writing about the first brick, and the second brick, and then by the third brick it all started to come and I couldn't stop. They thought I was crazy, and they kept kidding me, but here it all is. I don't understand it."

Neither did he, but on long walks through the streets of town he thought about it and concluded she was evidently stopped with the same kind of blockage that had paralysed him on his first day of teaching. She was blocked because she was trying to repeat, in her writing, things she had already heard, just as on the first day he had tried to repeat things he had already decided to say. She couldn't think of anything to write about Bozeman because she couldn't recall anything she had heard worth repeating. She was strangely unaware that she could look and see freshly for herself, as she wrote, without primary regard for what had been said before. The narrowing down to one brick destroyed the blockage because it was so obvious she had to do some original and direct seeing.

Focus on the Present, That's Key

In a Zendo, the Master teaches this to his disciples by assigning work. We call it Samu. Over the past 13 years, I have been assigned all kinds of work: sweeping the inner courtyard and the outer areas, mopping, gardening, taking care of the sand garden, cutting vegetables, dishwashing and cleaning restrooms. Most of the Zen students rush to see the notice board to see what they have been allotted and either get elated or completely disheartened. I remember the day I was assigned to wash dishes after lunch. The kitchen staff cooks for some 35students + 10 staff. I almost fainted when I saw the sink and the huge side table with all those vessels, cutting boards etc. A much older German gentleman with whom I was supposed to do the task, looked at my face and asked me if it was the first time I had been assigned this samu. When I answered yes, he took out his phone and showed me a short YouTube video- of Alan Watts talking about dishwashing. And it changed the way I looked at dishwashing forever.

AlanWatts is one of the best raconteurs of Zen. In my view, no one even comes close, leave alone at par with Alan Watts on prose or delivery of it. Hence, I would request you to watch that video. In that he teaches us again what is taught in Zazen meditation. We get disheartened by our memories of the past and future expectations. The moment we focus on the present, anything becomes a joyous activity. Even dish washing.

https://www.youtube.com/watch?v=Qx4fUpalvTU

There is a wonderful movie named *The Karate Kid* made in 1984. There is a newer version of the movie where Jackie Chan stars. However, in my opinion, the original where Pat Morita was Mr. Miyagi is a class apart. It's worth watching if you haven't seen it yet. I had shown that a few times to Manu and Rishi. In fact, it is a semi-autobiographical story based on the life of its screenwriter Robert Mark Kamen. When Robert was 17 years old, he faced a similar situation in New York.

In the movie Daniel, who gets bullied and beaten, asks Miyagi to teach him karate.And Miyagi starts his training by instructing the boy to do menial tasks like cleaning. One of the cult scenes of that movie, "wax on, wax off" reshaped the simple motion of polishing a car into the action of martial arts. Daniel initially didn't want to do the menial tasks. He wanted to quit. And when Miyagi made him understand how those menial tasks transformed into beautiful karate actions, Daniel's transformation began. As the old quote from Websters,

"Nothing is profane that serveth to holy things."

– Undefined

Most probably K.V. Kamath knew that and the understudy / intern from IIM did not.

Living in the Here and Now

If you think living in the present moment is all spiritual balderdash, let me give you an example from competitive sports. Nothing is played with more high stakes than competitive spectator sports in this world now.

This is Roger Federer talking about focusing on the moment and current point. While addressing graduates of Dartmouth college, Fedex said, "When you're playing a point, it has to be the most important thing in the world, and it is. But when it's behind you, it's behind you. That is regardless of where it is played, whether it is the first round of an obscure tournament, or the final of Wimbledon."

https://www.youtube.com/watch?v=pqWUuYTcG-o

That is the Zen way of being in the current moment. You don't worry about the past wins or losses, neither are you concerned about the future, you are with the current point. If one must be in that state, one has to rewire his brain and get out of the prison of value and fear.

In a way it does not matter whether you are playing in a competitive sport, or just preparing a routine mail to be posted to a few clients, ringing shokei or mokygyo, cutting vegetables or cleaning dishes, they are all exercises to empt your mind and be aware of our true self. That is the only lesson one learns from Zen. But that lesson takes a lifetime to learn.

(With due apologies to Robert Pirsig. I have read, read and reread that book, while the second book he wrote *Lila* stayed untouched in my bookshelf for over 25 years. When I started getting quotes, punch lines etc. from that book on the tip of my tongue, I realised it has become etched in my mind. This blog, in a sense, is a catharsis for me to empty my mind! Again, this is a long litany of ideas, hopping from one to another, like a butterfly in the garden of ideas. I hope you were motivated enough to stay until the last word.)

Chapter 13

Jackie Mu

The Zendog at Little Flower Zendo

The first dog in my life was the fictional hero in Jack London's *TheCall of the Wild*. His name was Buck. In that wonderful story, Jack Thornton saves Buck from being beaten to death and becomes his friend and master. I've read the translated version of the book umpteen times. The book had come with a few other good books as a prize for winning a quiz competition conducted by Kerala Sasthra

Sahitya Parishad. Buck's picture, a mix of St. Bernard and sheepdog, remains etched in my memory as if carved in stone. Thanks to JackLondon, who was a great storyteller. Years later, in 2020, a Hollywood movie was made with Harrison Ford as Jack Thornton. It was a good movie but the novel was better. Perhaps I read the book too many times at a very impressionable age.

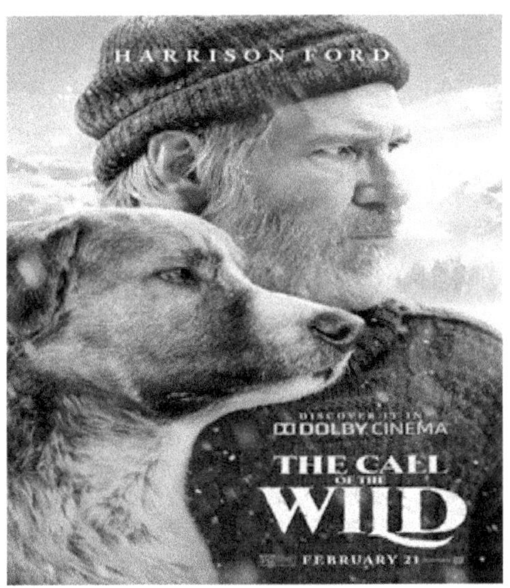

During my childhood in Thenkara, we—Sasi, Sandhya and I—adopted an Indian mongrel and named him Jackie. He was a wonderful dog with a great temperament. I can still recall the majestic way he rested on one of the pillars of our gate and gazed at the road. Once Jackie passed away, there was no other dog in our lives.

Years later, when Thara and I got married, she showed me a photo album full of pictures of their pet dogs.However, when Rishi and. Manu wanted to bring home a pet, Thara vetoed it saying that confining a dog to an apartment is like putting them in prison. Besides, in her considered view, the tiled floors do not suit dogs.

Coming to more recent times.I have been regularly going to Little Flower Zendo since January 2023.There was a friendly street dog there. She may have been a cross between an Indie and a hound, one of the estate guard dogs. She looked majestic and behaved like a hound.

She was soon adopted by Tithy, a long-time resident of Zendo and originally from Delhi. Tithy was an ardent dog lover and she took great care ofJackie Mu. Watching them was like imagining Joy Adamson taking care of the majestic Elsa. She was served dog food and snacks, she had a cozy bed and blanket, was taken to the vet regularly, was given regular baths and she even had her own medicine kit. When we went to the Zendo room for our early morningZazen, it was quite a sight watching Jackie Mu walking around with a blanket around her. She would be looking for someone to help her take off the blanket.

The dog had many names Jackie, Laddo etc. We added the surname Mu to her name when we got a special name plate for her. Mu is the most important Zen kōan. Mu was the first kōan in the book *The Gateless Gate*. Though the "Sound of one hand clapping" appears to be more popular and the most quoted in articles about Zen and kōans, in my view, Mu is the most important. It goes like this.

The 8th century Chinese Zen Master, whose Japanese name is Jôshû, was asked by a monk in all earnestness, "Can a dog have a Buddha-like nature?" Mu Jôshû said, "Mu (無)!" which can mean "nothingness." Without a doubt, Jackie Mu had a Buddha-like nature.

She was one of the wisest and smartest canines I knew. Better than Jack London's Buck. Out of the 15 odd rooms in Zendo, she knew which door to knock at for food, whom to be friendly with and from whom she should stay away.

Jackie Mu was my morning walk guide. She knew the way from Little Flower Zendo to Bodhi Zendo, a good 3.5 km through the main ghat road followed by estate roads. She would run ahead and show me the way. She would then wait at every turning and wait for me to catchup. And on the way back, we would stop at Surya, the roadside tea stall just opposite the St. Thomas Church. I would have tea and she would have biscuits.

After Tithy returned toDelhi, Jackie Mu looked lost for quite a few days. Even cookies and snacks didn't appeal much. There was quite a bit of pressure from some of the others to keep the dog out of the Zendo. According to them, she had become slightly aggressive. Perhaps she started feeling less cared for. Fr. AMA told me that at 89, he was too old and there was just no one else to take care of her. And I was at Zendo only for a week each month. Still, whenever I reached the Zendo after every 3weeks, her overjoyed reception said it all. During my short stay, she would shift her place at the Zendo to whichever floor and room I stayed in . And she kind of started following me wherever I went.

Her eager head would pop up in the verandah the moment the Zendo bells rang for the end of Zazen. And at sharp 7:30 am, the moment our breakfast finished, she would be ready for our morning walk. The stretching was her signal for us to be ready for the walk.

Some time back, at 9:37 pm I received this message on WhatsApp. "Vishy, I was just informed that Jackie Mu passed away yesterday. I am so sorry. I don't have more details." And when I called up Zendo, they told me that when she had come to Zendo in the afternoon, there was blood oozing from her nose. She lay down at her favourite place just outside the meditation hall and peacefully breathed her last.

I felt a pang in my heart.The last time I felt that way was when my ex-boss SMR passed away. As if some part deep within me died. Before receiving Jackie's news, I had been penning my daily three blessings before I hit the bed. And I just wrote this note asa tribute to one of my pals. Mahayana Buddhism does not believe in a soul per se. And I am sure, Jackie Mu would have left hers behind at the Zendo.

I wrote to Fr. AMA . "Dear Fr. AMA, Tithy messaged me at 9 37 pm saying. "Laddo / Jackie. Mu passed away." Suddenly I felt a pang in my heart. As something within me had died down. And I just happened to remember the koan . Mu. As you used to teach us, all beings are connected in a way." And replied very early morning next day. "I too was saddened by the death of Laadu. It was fond of you, followed you often. I am in tears. Peace to Laadu and to you and to me. Ama Samy."

On the morning of 20 July,Saturday, when I will be walking down the steep numberless steps to Zendo, I will miss the overjoyed welcome party of wet nose and holy presence of unconditional love from Buddha Nature.

Chapter 14

Surreal Tunes from a Broken Violin

21 March 2010

Ever since I moved into Tranquil, an apartment complex on Kanakapura Road, a refreshing Sunday practice included an early morning walk through Lalbagh with three of my friends, followed by breakfast atone of the popular cafés around Jayanagar. Among all the cafés, Maiyas is my favorite, though we always choose our café quite democratically! We usually stick to this positive routine unless someone in the pack has something more interesting or important to do on Sundays. On this particular Sunday, our outing was canceled since Sheik Iyer, the de facto and de jure leader of the pack, was catching an early morning train to Chennai. "Sheik", by his sheer personality and appearance—he was over 6 ft tall, athletic and lean at 40, clean shaven—looked like a Zen monk. Because of his honest and sincere approach and unparalleled commitment to purpose, he is our leader at the Tranquil community too. He made an effortless transition from being the Sr Corporate leader of a Middle Eastern conglomerate, with a fat pay cheque, a mansion and a fancy SUV, to a scooter-riding, FabIndia-clad social worker. Blessed with Buddhist equanimity, he is already quite a legend. Or at least one in the making.

Manu: My Little Buddha

I forced my offer of an early morning ride to the station over his protests, so that I could find some time alone at Lalbagh on my way back. I thought a couple of hours of solitude might help me get over the bruises of a recent event in my life. It really wasn't much to talk about, but the sheer hypocrisy and unfairness, convoluting insensitivity and lack of concern shown by people who matter saddened me a bit. Maybe just a bit, that many didn't even recognise it beneath my toothy forced smile. Except my little Buddha Manu. The most compassionate soul on Earth after the original one left this place some 2000 years ago, announced in his concerned tone "Papa you look sad," while offering a piece from his Cadbury's bar. Now Manu is someone who's usually very careful not to share his chocolates and sweets lest it might hurt the other's dental health!

Morning Magic at Lalbagh Botanical Garden

It was pitch black at Lalbagh at 5:30 am. The street lights had been turned off too. I didn't really want to take a chance with my delicate ankles so I chose to sit near the lake and meditate. An hour would have passed in a jiffy. But the experience was quite deep and the tides in my mind's muddied lake had calmed down. I came out of my meditation listening to a keerthana being played on a violin. The melodious music was like a soothing balm to my mind. The rising sun's rays and the cool morning breeze added to the magic. It was a moment with an ethereal quality. It is moments such as these that make the world beautiful and liveable. Humans probably invented art, music and meditation just for this and not for salvation to reach a place called heaven. Anyway many want to be there without dying and a few blow themselves up to reach quicker!

Guruprasad Rao, a connoisseur of Carnatic music and a good pal had told me many times that there used to be lovely concerts atLalbagh during the early morning hours. Leaving my usual walk trail, I trudged towards the bandstand through the south side of the Rose Garden to my first concert at Lalbagh. The violinist, a young girl, had already moved on to *Valiya Nayagane*. There were just a handful of people around the bandstand and their reactions to the music revealed their good knowledge about music. It seemed the size of the audience did not really matter to the young musician. She might have been playing for the roses, the birds, the giant cotton tree and the almighty spirit which connects all of them. In that state of mind and at that moment, I thought she was no less a violinist than L. Subramaniam or Kunnakudi Vaidyanathan, and frankly, the Lalbagh bandstand to me was no less than Prince Albert Hall or Shanmukhananda Hall.

Maybe it is another of those interesting coincidences or play of providence but later in the day, I reread a story thatl had read for the first time many years ago. It was from the book AlphaLeadership: Tools for Business Leaders Who Want More from Lifeby Ann Deering and RobertDilts. I have used this story umpteen number of times in my toastmaster speeches. I still find it relevant and refreshing and worth quoting verbatim.

"In November 1995, the violinist Itzhak Perlman performed at the Lincoln Center in New York City. He had polio as a child and walks with crutches. The audience waited patiently as he made his way slowly across the stage to his chair, sat down, put his crutches on the floor, removed the braces from his legs, settled himself in his characteristic pose, one foot tucked back, the other pushed forwards, bent down to pick up his violin, gripped it with his chin, and nodded to the conductor to indicate he was ready.

"It was a familiar ritual for Perlman fans: the crippled genius making light of his disability before his sublime music transcended everything. But this time was different."

"Just as he finished the first few bars," the *Houston Chronicle* music critic recalls, "one of the strings on his violin broke. You could hear it snap—it went off like gunfire across the room. There was no mistaking what that sound meant. There was no mistaking what he had todo." It was obvious, he had to put down his violin, replace his braces, pick up the crutches, heave himself to his feet, make his laborious way offstage and either get another violin or restring his crippled instrument."

"He didn't. He closed his eyes for a moment, and then signalled the conductor to begin again. The audience was spell-bound.

"Everyone knows it is impossible to play a symphonic work with just three strings. I know that, and you know that, but that night Itzhak Perlman refused to know that. He played with such passion and such power and such purity. You could see him modulating, changing, and recomposing the piece in his head. At one point it sounded like he was de-tuning the strings to get sounds from them they had never made before.

"When he finished there was an awed silence, and then the audience rose, as one.

"We were all on our feet, screaming and cheering—doing everything that we could to show him how much we appreciated what he'd done. He smiled, wiped the sweat from his brow, raised his bow to quiet us, and then he said, not boastfully, but in a quiet, pensive, reverent tone, 'You know, sometimes it is the artist's task to find out how much music he can still make with what he has left.'"

My Symphony

I had to take my own broken-stringed violin, which I would have probably touched just for a few hours in the last decade, to the shop at 8th Cross, 8th Main in Jayanagar 2nd Block. In the usual corporate style sales talk to build rapport, I asked him the price of a new violin. In his inimitable way, the owner of the shop replied that even though he had violins which cost up to Rs. 25,000, my present one was a really good one.

He took just Rs. 50 and 5 minutes to fix my violin. I might take a little while longer. A symphony is overdue with or without broken strings.

Chapter 15

Love + Logic = Light

24 August 2009

This is the story of two utter failures and the many half baked successes that I've seen in recent times. Now notions of success and failure inevitably bring in thoughts of pass marks and test papers. In my case, the complete credit for that self examination belongs to Dr. Richard McHugh, venerable NLP Guru. It was Dr. McHugh who drilled into my birdbrain the most important concept I learned (still learning!) about the art of communication. The idea: "The meaning of our communication is the response we get and there are no resistant listeners, only inflexible speakers," was quite difficult to grasp and even more difficult to practice. It was almost like watching the final scene of an Alfred Hitchcock movie at the start of the movie itself.

Let us delve into my stories of success and failure. I must emphasise on the word "stories" rather than "incidents", as that was another concept Dr. McHugh taught us. Any perception of a human being is a story and history is nothing but his/her story. So here we go.

Failures and Realisations

Even though the two protagonists of the first part of the story were as different as chalk and cheese, there were many striking similarities in their temperament, their world view and their approach to life. I knew them for quite some time and it was quite bizarre that most of the communication between us happened through emails. Also I am keen to add, that though the available evidences seems to suggest otherwise, both of them assumed they were perfectly right in all matters of contention, and the position of the undersigned or for that matter anyone else always lay in the realm of red or black (in their HUMBLE view). I should limit my descriptions of them so that their identities are not compromised at all. It is not really important to know who these folks are. It would be enough to know that in my own self righteous way, I quietly accepted many personal snide remarks in emails from them, before reacting or responding in a clinical fashion, like a surgeon. The only difference being that while surgeons administer anaesthesia before wielding their scalpels, my innocuous remarks loaded with subliminal messages reached their brains when they were absolutely conscious! Usually when I do that, I justify to myself—remembering Krishna's Shishupala story where the Lord forgave 100 insults before hitting out, and Jesus's mandate that we have to forgive 70 times 7. In my opinion, the fact that my cut off point could be counted in one hand—since I am an ordinary mortal—was quite liberal. The way the recipients recoiled in violent fashion to those "innocuous remarks" gave the small dark and cold corner in my mind momentary satisfaction. Soon sanity prevailed when I realised that once again I had failed in the Dr. McHugh's litmus test of communication.

My Half-baked Successes

Now my half baked success stories. Not long ago, I negotiated with a hard nosed, smart builder to withdraw their demand for Rs. 55 thousand just before registration of my apartment. I had to really blow hot and cold with them for a few weeks, before they finally relented.

I get the most satisfaction when I am able to convince my sons about small things. Manu is four and a half years old while Rishi is two and a half and talking things over with them usually takes a longtime. While the theoretical part of whatever little I know comes from Dr. McHugh, the practical part of it I owe completely to Manu and Rishi. It is an altogether different matter that they have their way most of the time!

Insights

Last week, as I was reflecting on one such episode of communication that ended in utter failure, I noticed a pattern.

- Failures stemmed from ego, past baggage and impersonal email communication;

- Success came from one of two reasons: one, when the focus and purpose of communication was absolutely on the issue; or second, when there was absolute trust and love in the air. As it was the case with my kids.

  Regardless of the vast progress we human beings have made in all spheres in life, I believe the ways we think and act have not changed at all. So it is fascinating to note that even though there are voluminous texts and research papers on the art and science of persuasive communication, none have captured the essence of it as beautifully as Aristotle. He divided the means of persuasion into three categories: Ethos,Pathos and Logos.

- Ethos or ethical appeal implies convincing by the character of the author / speaker.

- Pathos means persuading by appealing to the listener's emotions,

- Logos means persuading by the use of reasoning.

Ethos can be considered as the base ingredient, since without it no persuasion or communication ever happens. As Emerson rightly put it, "What you are, speaks so loudly, I can't even hear you speaking".

Empathy: A Tough Skill

I believe all of us have a door in our heart that can only be opened from inside. Most sensible people leave the door a bit ajar, they open it all the way only when they feel they are being understood perfectly. The kind knock at that door can be termed as empathetic listening or love. When the door is opened slightly, that is the time to put on our thinking cap and present the data, analysis and logic.

Without the initial empathetic listening, none of our logic reaches its intended target.

When it works out well, that is when you see the light bulb shining brightly on the listener's head.

As I found from my own experience, the toughest part is empathetic listening. The number of impediments to this can be quite long. Past history between the actors in the communication, our own ego, impatience, lack of time, the basic need in each of us to be heard and a tendency to hog the air waves, all can force the door at the heart that the listener closes tightly. Also we need to be aware that by being empathetic, we are agreeing, nor conceding, any ground with respect to views. We are just acknowledging with respect, that his/her viewpoint may have merit in it. Our own conduct in empathetic listening, by being patient, by being respectful and by acknowledging is what opens the door in the heart. Once the door opens, one doesn't have to be a Cicero to convey the message.

Chapter 16

Untied for Humanity!

3 September 2024

Way back in 2012, I had a wonderful opportunity to travel for work to Johannesburg, South Africa, twice in two months. Those travels are etched in my mind for many reasons. I traveled to Joburg shortly after the South Africa Police Force opened fire on protesting workers who had been on strike demanding a wage raise. Many were killed. The incident became notorious as the Marikana Massacre.

Rosebank Square, which was very close to our hotel, was a wonderful place where many amateur but superb musical groups performed during weekends. I still remember the performance by a young group from the ghettos of Soweto. That year I was lapping up books on the Adamsons (Joy and George) and Lawrence Antony, the famous conservationist who wrote that wonderful book *The Elephant Whisperer*. Last but not the least important reason was my friendship with Terrence of Terrie's taxi. Kaushik Sanyal, my manager then at Wipro Consulting, had been to Joburg before. He told me that Joburg was a crime-ridden place and the best way to be safe and secure was to go with Terrie.

Terrie was a wonderful person. The moment he realised that I was from South India, he put on a Tamil FM station as he drove me from the airport to the hotel. His style of connecting with his customers was a masterclass in communication. In fact, I'm still connected with Terrie on Facebook—for over 12 years now— and we wish each other on our birthdays and other occasions. The same goes for my ex-boss Kaushik Sanyal who is a dear friend but we haven't met for many many years!

At that time the only South African leader I knew of was Nelson Mandela. But Terrie spoke mostly about Desmond Tutu. As I read further, I understood that while Nelson Mandela was the key figurehead in the fight against apartheid, Desmond Tutu was the soul of South Africa. Tutu did not stop his fight for humanity even after apartheid was abolished in the RSA. He continued to voice and act for the betterment of the oppressed across the world in his own compassionate way.

A few years before that, I worked in a major bellwether IT company in Bangalore. They were the poster boys of the Indian IT world. They had a Disney World kind of campus in Bangalore and they took the upkeep of that campus very seriously. At almost any time of the day, you would see housekeeping staff cleaning and looking for invisible dirt on the walkways. I called it Disney World because the campus had all kinds of strange looking glass buildings. They probably still do.

Another aspect of that life was the "tie" culture. They took it very seriously. Twice a week, a tie was compulsory. The HR head thought that wearing a tie was the only way one can be and look professional. By tying you down! Security guards were instructed to keep track of all the male employees who violated the Tie Code. The rule-breakers were then fined; Rs 200 was deducted from your salary. To be fair, that Tie Code was applicable to all, from the top to the bottom. Now, I had an allergy to anything that tied me down and I always tried to avoid wearing a tie.

Relationships Matter

From my early days at Wipro, I had made it a habit to wish and connect with all our guards, the receptionist and the boy who made and served us tea at the M.G. Road office. There was a legendary story, that the Tea Master was so famous for his tea that when Mindtree opened their first building in Banashankari, Ashok Soota ensured he too joined their pantry. Once when Kalyan Kumar

Banerjee, the Mindtree HR head, invited us to their office to initiate a Toastmasters Club, I met the TeaMaster there.

I probably learnt to treat everyone with courtesy, regardless of their position, from R Bala, one of my early bosses at Wipro. He headed the IBM UK account. When Bala led a small team to Germany for a pilot project, I was one of the fabulous four selected for that trip. Bala had a way of connecting with everyone regardless of hierarchy and he treated each one of us with the same care and compassion. Maybe that is one of the reasons I still stay connected with him and call him occasionally. Regardless of whether he is in Bangalore or London, he answers the call and still talks to me in the same manner. Incidentally, when we worked together on that project in Ludwigsburg, I didn't know how to tie a tie and he taught me. He also taught us PL/1, a programming language in Mainframe, which was the mainstay of our client's programs.

That habit of staying in touch continued at the "Disney World company" too. And the staff never noted my employee ID and I never got fined. However, that became an issue in another way for me. My boss there, who usually dressed very properly, got fined once and as he shared the fact, a teammate pointed out that I never wore a tie. When asked, in my utter foolishness, I shared my secret very euphorically. Everyone else in that meeting room had a hearty laugh. But I later realised that it was the start of my trouble there.

This morning, there was a pleasant incident as I walked into the office. A wonderful flower arrangement.

That reminded me about Little Flower Zendo. A few months ago, I was allocated the work of cleaning the meditation hall and taking care of the flower arrangement at Zendo. Cleaning was easy, but flower arrangements! So, I took help from Surya, a Korean national and a longtime resident of Auroville. She is excellent at calligraphy and ikebana! Her work was wonderful, and ikebana is almost meditative.

So, when I saw the similar pattern at the Wipro front office that day, I wrote a small note and asked the receptionist to hand it over to the person who did this every other day. Isn't it wonderful to see such an arrangement as you enter the workplace? Now Thara and I do one at home as well. And every ikebana is beautiful. S/he seems to have replied with that arrangement. The receptionist later told me that in all her years of working there as a receptionist, this was the first time someone had left a note of appreciation for the person who made the floral arrangement!

Ikebana arrangement by Mustafa at Little Flower Zendo

We, with our discriminating judgmental minds, value one and undervalue another. At the end of the day, what difference does it make whether it is a billionaire or someone else who does an ikebana arrangement to make a living?

By the way, you won't believe it. The flower arrangement was done by Bhagya Lakshmi, a young housekeeping staff member. Today the receptionist introduced me to Bhagya and she thanked me for my note of appreciation.

As the saying goes, there are some things in life that money can't buy, for everything else, there's Mastercard!

All of us would have read that "chicken soup for the soul" story about a college professor giving his class a quiz. The last question of the test was, "What is the name of the woman who cleans your classroom?" A student asked the professor whether the question would count toward the quiz grade.

"Absolutely," said the professor. "In your careers, you will meet many people. All are significant. They deserve your attention and care, even if all you do is smile and say hello."

I would change the word career to life. In life, we meet many people. All are significant. They deserve our attention and care.

Desmond Tutu once said "My humanity is bound up in yours, for we can only be human together."

There are a lot of layers of meaning and spiritual essence in that one quote. It is almost like the Zen Kōan "The sound of one hand clapping."

Chapter 17

Prince Aslan and Manu in the World of Narnia

Prince Aslan. Pic Courtsey: https://www.pinterest.com/ pin/6122149487722337/

I was trying to watch one of those meaninglessChinese martial arts movies over the weekend. I turned it off when I realised I was missing Manu's presence. Manu was in Mysore for his well earned vacation after all the "hardwork" he had put in at his Montessori, karate, chess and painting classes. He still had enough energy to fight with Rishi, his younger brother and ransack my bookshelf. Watching a movie together was a routine that began quite recently. One Saturday night, as I was putting away a book I was trying to read, I realised that Manu was still watching TV.

The moment he saw my shadow, he had his plea ready, all coated with that sweet 1000 W smile. "Papa, this is not a cartoon. It's Narnia, why don't you watch it? It's good." My four-and-a-half year old son is well aware of his parent's concern over his overindulgence in the world of Power Rangers, Spiderman and Ben 10. I couldn't say no to the best salesman in the world, even though I shy away from watching movies that are based on good books that I have read and liked. The only exceptions probably were *Godfather* and *Gone with the Wind*. This was the *Chronicles of Narnia*.

The movie had almost finished. There was a scene when the trees started moving to help the protagonists. And I tried enlightening my son about the rational aspects of the world, "It is just a movie and trees can't move." He looked at me, quite amused at my incredulity, and chastised me saying "Papa, when a lion can speak English, trees can run too." Now that logic was watertight; I didn't have an answer to that. For the rest of the movie, I just watched. The punch line was yet to be delivered. The moment the final scene was over, when the protagonists were transposed back to the London Underground station, he got up and announced, "Magic is over and it's time to sleep."

Even though I am quite aware that human brains are wired to distinguish between a photograph and an actual person, a movie and real stuff, I felt it was quite incredible that such a young kid could make sense of it so intuitively. Let me assure you, I am not one of those eager beaver kind of parents who wants to make his kid a scientist as early as possible.

As Buckminster Fuller had written, "All children are born geniuses. 9,999 out of every 10,000 are swiftly, inadvertently de-geniused by grown-ups."

And it is not just about Manu. If we really look around, it is not that difficult to notice the great innate light of talent and inborn wisdom in almost all kids we come across. That light starts fading when they start formal schooling. When Thara and I were looking for a place to stay, the only criterion we had was that we should live in a place that had an offbeat school in the neighbourhood. And that's how we settled down on Kanakapura Road. Even though there are many things we don't agree about, one of the things we did agree about was that, whatever the circumstances, we do not want our kids to live their lives to fulfil our own unfinished script, our unfulfilled ambitions, or to rewrite the stories of our failures and half successes. We don't want them to live out the remaining part of our lives. We wanted them to chart their own course and write their own scripts, creating magic in their own Narnia worlds.

Chapter 18

MedIT-action and in-NO-OVATION: whyZEN for kaiZEN?

2 August 2024

Frederik G. Pferdt was the first ever Chief InnovationEvangelist of Google. He recently published a book, *What's Next Is Now: How to Live Future Ready.* According to him, the book can help anyone to live a more meaningful life. I highly recommend the book to everyone.

Especially the last point: "Spend time with yourself."

The book emphasises the importance of taking breaks on a regular basis, just to be with yourself. It is not about taking a vacation with family and friends. Rather, it's about taking time to be just with yourself. More frequently.

There is a famous quote by Franz Kafka, "You do not need to leave your room. Remain sitting at your table and listen. Do not even listen, simply wait, be quiet, still and solitary. The world will freely offer itself to you to be unmasked, it has no choice, it will roll in ecstasy at your feet." French philosopher and mathematician Pascal too wrote, "All of humanity's problems stem from man's inability to sit quietly in a room alone."

Incidentally, some 30 years ago, I learnt computer programming in Pascal and Turbo Pascal, and today Kafka is a data streaming platform.

Pferdt says that meditating every day helps to keep him open to new ideas and steer away from negativity.

The word "MEDITate" means to focus one's thoughts, to reflect on or to ponder over. And the word "ACTION" means the state of acting for a specific purpose. In today's world, there are as many types of meditation as there are human perspectives. And currently, "mindfulness" seems to be the most used/overused/abused term, at least in corporate circles, especially ever since Zen reached the western shores during the early 20th century.

For many in the western world, hardwired in their brain with that dry logic of Aristotle, is the fact that mindfulness and meditation are just means to meet some other ends. A de-stressor, productivity enhancer and some soothing balm for their tired nerves. But for an oriental, who has grown up in the cradle of Patanjali, Buddha, Nagarjuna, Bodhidharma, Tao and Zen, the journey is the destination. The path is made by walking on it. And salvation/realisation is here and now. It lies at the meeting point of eternal and temporal, doing and do-nothing, action and inaction and between breathing inspiration (in breath) and expiration (out breath). Aspiration, a strong desire to achieve something else, is not just a medical risk but a hindrance to a spiritual seeker as well.

My Journey Along the Path of Spirituality and Meditation

I have been a student of spirituality and meditation for over 30 years. I have read quite a bit and done my share of channel surfing and spiritual shopping. In fact, Late Dr. Satish Inamdar, KFI Trustee and Director of The Valley School, had once said to me that I would find my "way" when I stopped reading so much!

The seeds of Zen were planted in my mind in June, 1998 at the unlikeliest of places—West Haven. It was my first visit to the land of baseball and basketball. As a spectator, both games were like Greek and Latin to me. In the NBA finals, the Chicago Bulls were playing against the Utah Jazz. What caught my eye and attention was Coach Phil Jackson of the Chicago Bulls. I had read an interesting article in

The New York Times about him. He had managed players like Dennis Rodman, who was an out and out rebellious and rule breaking toughie, Scottie Pippen and the larger-than-life Michael Jordan. I have read and reread his book *Sacred Hoops* more than once. He was deeply spiritual with Native Indian and Zen philosophy ingrained in him. In fact, Jackson spent a large part of his life studying Buddhism and its principles under his mentor Shun Ryu Suzuki.

Jackson wrote,

"What appealed to me about Zen practice was its inherent simplicity. It didn't involve chanting mantras or visualising complex images, as had other practices I'd tried. Zen is pragmatic, down-to-earth, and open to exploration. It doesn't require you to subscribe to a certain set of principles or take anything on faith."

– Phil Jackson, Coach of Chicago Bulls
and LA Lakers

Pic courtesy: https://twitter.com/TheDunkCentral

Over 14 years later, in 2012, after my own experiments with truth and lies of spirituality, I made a hard landing at Bodhi Zendo and Zen and that's when my real spiritual journey began.

AMA Samy and Bodhi Zendo were different. I would compare Bodhi Zendo a little bit with the Esalen Institute at Big Sur, California.

Bodhi Zendo is one of the most beautiful places of learning that I have visited. It is not as regimented as a Vipassana session, it gives a good amount of personal space to everyone. Sometimes a good conversation, a good joke and laughter at the dining table along with some delicious food is as enriching as anything else in this world while seeking spirituality. There are many who were/are very serious seekers. And then there were the many others. Some had made it their very affordable summer resort to get away from the Pondicherry or Chennai summer. They were so full to the brim with Aurobindo or other thought leaders that it was quite doubtful that they had any space in their mind for Zen. In fact, Zen is about the empty mind and nothingness and does not add anything more to us.

Secondly, AMA Samy has one of the best collections of books on spirituality, philosophy, theology and psychology. AMA seems to have read most of them. When I was a full time student of MA Education at Azim Premji University Bangalore, I had to write a term paper on the Phenomenology of Krishnamurti's teachings as an assignment for Dr. Kaustav Roy. I was searching for a book by Martin Heidegger at the Zendo library one December afternoon. AMA walked in to keep some book and he asked me what I was reading. When I explained to him my struggle with that Phenomenology paper, he spent15-20 mins summing it up for me like a precis. I ran back to my room and jotted down whatever I could remember. That assignment was one of the few for which I got an O grade. And getting that from Dr. Kaustav Roy was almost like winning a Fields Medal.

Third, and most importantly, no one demands the camel-has-to-pass-through-the-eye-of-the-needle test of faith first and salvation later. The Kālāma Sutta poster on the wall says it so succinctly, "Don't blindly believe what I say. Don't believe me because others convince you of my words. Don't believe anything you see, read, or hear from others, whether of authority, religious teachers or texts." And AMA Samy practices it completely, dotting every i and j and crossing every t. Though he had a tough and rough demeanour as a Zen master, there was an endearing quality of integrity and compassion about the man. He took his spirituality and teaching seriously, not himself. That was very refreshing to my tired seeking mind.

Even then, it took me three years of seeking to be accepted as AMA's Zen student. As the saying goes, once bitten twice shy and the cat that falls into a hot water tub will stay even in a cold water one. Heidi was a co-student of AMA in Japan with Yamada Roshi, and later became AMA Samy's student. She spoke to me and asked me to join Bodhi Sangha.

And I decided to seek to be accepted as a student of AMA Samy after reading this passage in one of the books written by him.

> *"The master cannot give you satori; she/ he is there to guide, to challenge, to test, to confirm. In truth, all the world is your teacher, the whole life of birth-and-death is the training field. The task of the Zen master is not to teach self-being but to convey that it cannot be taught, that no methodology is capable of bringing it about. By forcing the student to look within herself/himself, however, for that mode which (though unactualised) has been there all along, the Zen master may be said to be teaching.This teaching which is a non-teaching is Zen's most unique pedagogy. Rarely will a Zen master say what Zen is but will inexorably express what it is not.Zen, therefore, is a teaching by negation, negating everything that the student supposes Zen to be, hoping that the student will realize that by not being any particular thing, s/he is everything; and that by not being any particular self, s/he is selflessly all selves. Negation, thus, is an affirmation which is not acquired but which happens, which is awakened as naturally as ordinary consciousness, as though it had been there all along."*
>
> *– Undefined*

I won't venture into a personal account of the merits and demerits of other spiritual teachers and their teachings. I believe in the dictum, to each his/her own. And my better half Thara has clearly taught me that, "What is good for the goose, may not be good for the gander." In fact, if Nitya Chaitanya Yati or Eknath Easwaran were alive, I would have sought them out. I would have crossed a desert or swam across an ocean to learn from them. At the same time, I stay away from a few, though I live a walking distance away from where they "teach."

I have been a student of AMA Samy for more than nine years now and since Jan 2023, I made it a point to be at the Little Flower Zendo, Perumalmalai, Kodaikanal, at least once a month.

Commend and recommend: Zen, AMA Samy and https://littleflowerzendo.in. That is the most Zen-like reference one Zen student can offer to one's dear and near.

Fr AMA Samy , Zen Master and Founder Bodhi Sangha

Chapter 19

Freedom or Free-Doom?

"One morning an irresistible force propelled MIT professor, Marvin Minsky to one corner of his classroom and pinned him here as securely as a butterfly impaled in a museum showcase. It was the force of habit – a brand new habit imposed upon him on the spot by a group of playfully experimental students. The boys had him at their mercy, as if he was a robot slave and they, the masters at the controls.

They 'robotized' Minsky with a psychological ruse much like the methods for teaching rats to run through a maze, or training a dog to fetch a newspaper. Soon after the class began, a few students started manipulating him. Whenever he paced to the right, they whispered softly to each other, rustled papers, dropped pencils, and created other minor distractions. But when he happened to take a few steps to the left, they sat up and paid close attention to the lecture. In short they conditioned Minsky by repeatedly punishing him for moving in one direction and rewarding him for moving in the opposite direction. Within half an hour he stopped pacing altogether and stood like a cigar store Indian near the left hand edge of the black board. So subtly had he been habituated that he did not realise an experiment was in progress, and that he was the guinea pig-ironically, since Minsky is a leading authority on the theory of automations." (Think, November – December 1969).

By all accounts, Minsky is not one of those ordinary Steves or Charlies. Minsky is listed on Google Directory as one of the all time top six people in the field of AI. Isaac Asimov described Minsky as one of only two people he would admit were more intelligent than himself, the other being Carl Sagan. Patrick Winston has also described Minsky as the smartest person he has ever met. That is some CV, I should say.

Now the pertinent question that rises is where does that leave us? i.e. You and me? When someone like Minsky was so easily susceptible to environmental conditioning, how free are we? Free will, Clear thinking, Seeing it as it is, Objectivity- are these just yearnings of a mind that is a prisoner of conditioning? Some of it is inherited from nature. And some of it is acquired through nurture.

Aren't we living the lives of somnolence, like programmed characters in a Shakespearian drama? Conditioned to see what we want to see, hear what we want to hear and feel what we want to feel.

Perhaps we fail to understand that these conditionings act as filters between us and the "Real world out there."

In all reality, it is in our arrogance, we added one of the many meanings of the word twist "to alter or distort the intended meaning of." It suggests that human beings do that only intentionally and deliberately. At all other times they seem to claim that they get the meaning as it is! As one of the best examples of cultural conditioning, it still holds out after some 2500 years of "experiential wisdom" of one Sidhartha Gautama who suggested it all starts with having the "right view". The *"Meaning of Meaning"* proposed by I.A. Richards, literally suggests that meaning resides in people and not in words. It all boils down to same. We create our own worlds in our brain, which could be an absolutely distorted version of the real World out there. The realisation that our own conditioning and filters Twist (the way I see that) and distort reality may be the signpost at the fork between freedom and free-doom.

Chapter 20

Classic Ends - Immortal Stories about Mortal Deaths

The most clichéd and boring statement I have heard during my time @Toastmasters was, "Public speaking is the most feared thing among the public, far above the fear of death or disease." I really don't know the basis of that statement. Probably most of the populace may be afraid of the prospect of public humiliation, considering the fact that our collective egos may cover the distance between earth and sun.

Incidentally I have never been afraid of public speaking, not even when I was learning to fly a little kite. I never thought much about death until my father passed away four years ago. Even when he was ushered into the operation theatre by a well known cardiothoracic surgeon in Bangalore – who said my father had one of the lowest risk rating in the Euro score- my father was calm and collected. After about four days he was the only one left in that 15-bed Surgical ICU and soon he had slipped into the unknown as graciously as he had lived, leaving us all behind. For some strange reason, as I stood beside his bed watching the attendants clean his body, I did not feel bereaved nor did I cry. My tears came much later.

Soon after that, I chanced upon a book titled "The Tibetan book of the Dead." I could never make much progress with the book for years. A few weeks ago, one of my wonderful colleagues-who is a rare species in the corporate jungle, a kind of Zen master or would-be saint-told me that it was really a good book. That brought that old dusty volume out of the book shelf into my reading list again. I also started jotting down the impressions I had in my mind from my readings on what else, classy deaths. Here I am, jotting down a few of them. I am retaining the original, for fear of killing the life in those wonderful lines.

Pic courtesy : Wikipedia

The first one has to be one of the Americans I admire a lot. Richard Feynman. When the Los Angeles times, sent him an advanced copy of his obituary, he thanked the author but said, "I have decided it is not a very good idea for a man to read it ahead of time, it takes the element of surprise out of it." He knew he was not recovering. He was 69. The cancer had relapsed. Pain wracked one of his legs. He was exhausted. In one corner of his dusty office blackboard at Caltech, he had written a pair of self conscious mottos and a running list under the heading "To Learn". He had not accumulated much: A hand knitted scarf, hung on a peg, a photograph of Michelle with her cello, some black and white pictures of aurora borealis, a van painted with chocolate brown Feynman diagrams. On Feb 3, he entered UCLA Medical center again. His functioning kidney had failed. One round of dialysis was done. Feynman refused further dialysis that might have prolonged his life for weeks or months. He told Michelle calmly,

"I am going to die." He had probably anticipated his own death, he told one of his friends "You see, one thing is, I can live with doubt and uncertainty and not knowing. I think it is much more interesting to live not knowing than to have answers that might be wrong. I have approximate answers and possible belief. I don't have to know the answer. I don't feel frightened by not knowing things, by being lost in a mysterious universe without any purpose, which is the way it really is as far as I can tell. It does not frighten me." He drifted towards unconsciousness. His eyes dimmed. Speech became an exertion. He drew himself together, prepared the last phrase and released it; "I hated having to die twice.It is so boring…" Soon he was gone.(Don't remember the title of the article from which i had quoted the above passage about Feynman. Duly acknowledging)

Then there is this one that I got it from the Outlook obituary of Bhimsen Joshi. Saba Naqvi writes about the death of Mallikarjun Mansur, the saintly Hindustani classical singer legend from Dharwar. "He had lung cancer. The doctors had given up. So his daughter was instructed not to keep him away from things he loved most. The last thing he asked for was a *bidi* to smoke. He was humming Raga Jogia, almost inaudibly. His daughter placed between his lips a lit *bidi*. And his head rolled over. He was gone. I told this story to Bhimsen Joshi. He heard the story with a distant look, smiled and a tear rolled down his cheek."

Mallikarjun Mansur at a concert. Picture courtesy Wikipedia

And continuing in the same story about the late Abdul Karim Khan.

"Singing at platforms links up nicely with a story from Abdul Karim Khan's life or rather his death.On his way to Puducherry at the invitation of Sri Aurobindo, Khan sahib had a premonition that his end was nearing. He left the train at an unknown railway station, spread out his prayer mat and sang his last song. He died on the railway platform. The news was carried to Sri Aurobindo by the disciples accompanying him. "

Let me end with the story of another American who was a constant presence in my life through the last page humour column of *The Hindu* for many years. Art Buchwald. He was a very popular humorist and political satirist whose work was syndicated in multiple American newspapers including The New York Times and The Washington Post. In addition to being a writer, he was also someone who apparently suffered from serious bouts of depression throughout his life. He died on last Wednesday, January 17, 2007 after a long illness and extended hospice care. Mr. Buchwald had the distinction of being the first person to pre-record his own video obituary for The New York Times. Far from being grim, this interview and documentary is quite uplifting, and I think, very much worth watching. The most important point in that videos is

Knowing that you are dying is no reason to stop living.

– Art Buchwald

"You may have to alter or adjust some of your previous activities, but there is no reason to shut down completely. If you can no longer read, find some books on tape, or have a family member read to you. If you can't type, have a person email or type for you, etc., etc. Consider reuniting with lost friends or forgiving old enemies. You don't have to be a famous columnist to pass on a legacy. Compose a letter or videotape your own interview to share your thoughts and life experiences with future generations. "

Until his very last day, Buchwald continued writing and hosted a lot of guests. "I'm having a swell time — the best time of my life" he quipped. I hope that the rest of us don't wait until we are dying to have such fun.

Chapter 21

Stopped Time and Frozen Tears

Maps in our mind and
borders in our heart

A sculpture made by S.L. Parasher during his time at the refugee camp in Baldev Nagar (1947–48) Ambala. Source: http://www.imgrum.org/user/partitionmuseum/3497128151/1566545348243402212

"While the image of the 'corpse train' arriving full of the dead and mutilated remains perhaps the most enduring icon of Partition, most passenger services had been halted after the initial attacks. The worst massacres only came to pass now. Over the weekend of September 20-21, four of the Pakistan Specials rolled across the border and into Lahore one after the other, their floors slick with blood. Some had been attacked multiple times. One train's escort had fended offa jatha in 45 minutes of ferocious hand-to-hand fighting. Another had lost several hundred passengers, including 62 children under the age of eight. OnSeptember 22, after a refugee train coming the other way arrived in Amritsar full of non-Muslim dead and wounded, the Sikh fighters went berserk. A mob estimated at 10,000 people swarmed a Pakistan-bound train full of Muslim refugees, firing automatic rifles, tossing bombs, and slashing away with swords. Only 200 horribly wounded passengers survived; at least 1,500 people were killed, including the British commander of the train's escort.Bourke-White arrived at the scene soon afterward. All along the platform, she later wrote, blue-turbaned Sikhs sat cross-legged, their curved kirpans across their knees, patiently waiting for the next arriving Special."

– An excerpt from Nisid Hajari's Midnight's Furies: The Deadly Legacy of India'sPartition

Thara, Rishi and I were at the Partition Museum, which is housed in the Amritsar Town Hall building. The red coloured sandstone building was an old British Commissionerate and jail. It is just a stone's throwaway from Jalianwala Bagh, the place that once witnessed one of the worst criminal acts by an army officer in recorded history. If one is sensitive enough, one can still hear the cries and commotion of the Jalianwala Bagh massacre, as Col. Reginald Dyer and his vulture army, opened fire at an innocent congregation of freedom fighters.

The roads between the Golden Temple, Jaliansala Bagh and the town hall is a pedestrian-only cobbled walkway. And what catches the eye is the standard shop signages that melt into the stone coloured building and huge statues of some remarkable Indians. If one can tolerate or ignore the number of touts who want to take you to the Wagah border ceremony, it is quite an enjoyable walk.

The Partition Museum seems to be a new addition, especially when compared with the Golden Temple and Jalianwala Bagh, both of which were witness to many generations of smiles and tears, sukoon and blood, and pride and prejudice. the museum portrays both the dark, hateful and demonic side of human nature along with Jalianwala Bagh and the humane side found at the Golden Temple.

The museum is the brain child of Mallika Ahluwalia, a Harvard graduate, whose paternal and maternal grandparents were tragic victims of the barbaric violence during the partition.

We had planned to make a quick round of the museum before lunch. Our driver Guri Saheb, a young, affable and devout Sardar reminded us he couldn't park in front of the Brothers Dhaba for too long. Both locals and tourists throng to the dhaba for their utterly butterly kulcha and piping hot channa!

We were just strolling through the halls, without paying too much attention to all the information about the politics of those times. It was more like an effort to tick off the museum in our tourist to-do list. We were kind of jolted when we reached the center of the Hall of Migration and Refugees. There was a small well that depicted the suicides committed by the many women who jumped into the well and killed themselves to save their honour during that incident. There was a beautiful phulkari dupatta draped across the walls near that well. The note said it was donated by one Mr. Randhawa, whose aunt was asked by her kith and kin to jump into the well and save herself being raped and killed. She chose not to take that step and was rescued by a Muslim man. This was one of the stories of kindness and humaneness shown by many across all communities in the midst of hatred, anger and bloodshed.

And just next to that was a booth that displayed the portraits created by Sardari LalParashar. How does one draw grief, loss, sadness, suffering? Parashar was an acclaimed painter, etcher, sculptor and writer on the other side of the divide before the lines were drawn on a piece of map.

A pencil sketch of Dr. Rabindra Nath Tagore by Mr. S.L. Prasher M. A., drawn while the Poet was listening to the music of Sikh minstrels. Dr. Tagore looked at the sketch and said, "Yes, you have got it. You have caught my expression. There is character and strength in it. I like it very much."

Source: S.L. Parashar 1904–1990, Time, Space,Light, Consciousness

After crossing over the blood-soaked border, Parashar's first job was as commandant in a refugee camp in Baldev Nagar, Ambala. He was overwhelmed by the pain, sorrow, fear and anguish of the inmates of the camp, all of those emotions creeped into his sketches. Those sketches tell the true story of the horrors of partition.

Even after all these years, the pain and suffering is still fresh in those sketches. I had to go back to the booth downstairs, to have a look again at Sir Cyril Radcliffe, the man who was primarily responsible for one of the worst manmade calamities in the world. Even the most conservative figures show the extreme depth to which humans can descend. A BBC article on the partition says, "About 12 million people became refugees. Between half a million and a million people were killed in religious violence. Tens of thousands of women were abducted."

Pic courtesy: BBC article on partition

W H Auden's poem, *Partition* displayed in the booth and it speaks only the part of the story about the main villain.

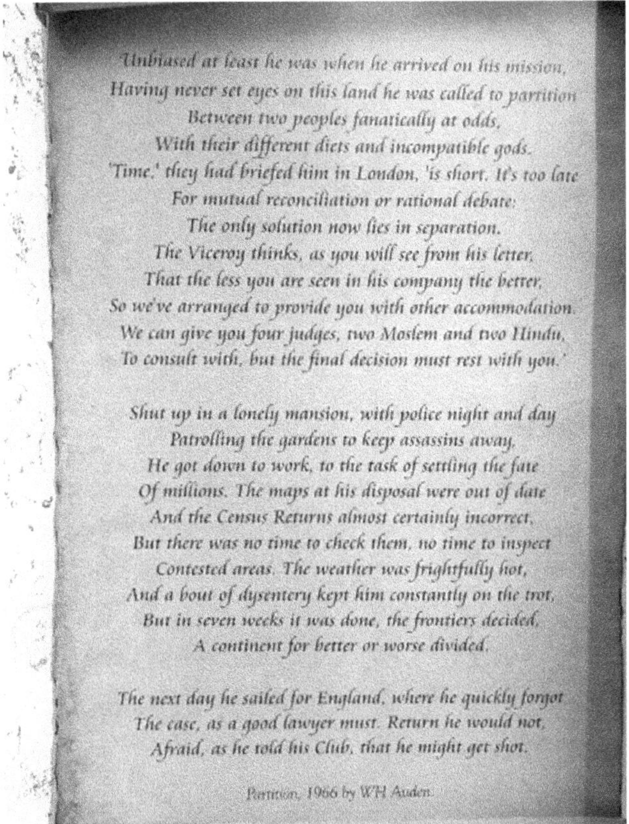

Poem on Partition by W.H. Auden. Pic courtesy: Partition Museum Amritsar

Let me quote from an interview of Radcliff by veteran journalist Kuldeep Nayar in 1976.

"To make an 'impartial' decision, the British chose English barrister Sir Cyril Radcliffe to draw the boundary that would demarcate the Punjab and Bengal provinces. Radcliffe had never visited British India or written about it ever in his professional life as a lawyer. He virtually had no knowledge of the subcontinent, which was why he was chosen as somebody who'd make an 'unbiased' decision.He was given two Muslim and Hindu Judges each to help in the task."

– Quote from an interview of Radcliff by veteran journalistKuldeep Nayyar in 1976.

So that's how the story of Radcliffe's line goes. An English barrister, who never set foot in India before July 8, 1947, decided which families would be part of India and which houses would go to East and West Pakistan.

"According to records, Radcliffe barely knew where Punjab and Bengal were, yet he accepted the job as a man with a deep sense of duty. In that interview, he reveals that he 'had almost given Lahore to India but was then told how Pakistan would be left without any major city' as the decision to give Calcutta to India was already taken."

In another corner of that book tells the story of the necklace from Mohenjo-Daro. "When the necklace was separated into two sections, Pakistan received a portion of six light-green jade beads and three agate-jasper pendants. Currently, this half of the necklace is on exhibit at the Mohenjo Daro Museum in Pakistan, while the other half is located in theNational Museum in New Delhi, India."

In the same interview with Nayar, he further said "The time at my disposal was so short that I could not do a better job. However, if I had two to three years, I might have improved on what I did." Five weeks-in just five weeks - the fate of millions of people got sealed and this unleashed an epic humanitarian crisis."

So saddened was Radcliffe to hear about the death of people on either side of the lines that he refused to accept payment for his work. Then that is the story of a lawyer who worked probono! I still wonder, why a person ever would undertake such a task with such hasty deadlines.

Thirty years after partition, Sir Cyril died in April 1977 in Britain. It is said that after drawing the 'Radcliffe Line,' he left India the very next day and never returned.

"That which passes, isn't time. You and I are transitory, time is eternal. Or rather, it passes and is yet eternal." —

– **Gulzar,** *Raavi Paar and Other Stories*
Undefined

The last section of the museum was the best part. The section of hope. The extraordinary story of ordinary people, who saw the worst of human nature yet chose to be good human beings. Those men excelled as human beings and transcended the slippery slope of hatred and anger. Milkha Singh, HeroMotors Munjal, Manmohan Singh and F.C. Kohli, the father of Indian IT industry. Manmohan Singh's taped voice spoke about how his grandfather was brutally murdered in cold blood in Peshawar and he, after crossing over to Amritsar after partition, studied for his Intermediate and BA at the Motilal Nehru Library which is located next door to the Town hall where the partition museum located. He could not afford to buy books and as a refugee, he could study only because his college waived his fees. The endless list goes on…. The seed of hatred takes root only on petty and weak hearts. The founder of the Partition Museum had written a wonderful book with 21 inspirational stories. There could be many more unheralded ones.

After penning a short note in the visitors book, it was time to go to the Wagah border show, which included the beating retreat or flag lowering ceremony. It seems that in the ancient days, a war started at the sunrise and ended at sunset. Remember the story in the *Sauptika Parva*, or the *Book of Sleepers*, the 10th book of the *Mahabharata*. After the 18th day of the war, three Kauravas led by Ashwatthama, entered the Pandava camp in the middle of the night and slaughtered the sleeping Pandava men. At the end, even after victory only eight Pandava men and three Kauravas remained alive. Ironically our driver told us that Wagah is on the Pakistan side of the border while the Indian side is known as Attari. I was left wondering why the patriotic Indians promote Pakistan! There was already a huge crowd waiting for the security check, to be let into the semicircular coliseum -style stadium facing the gate from the Indian side. There is a similar and smaller stadium on the other side. All of us were made to pass through a metallic detector and thoroughly frisked. The BSF jawans did not even let a cigar lighter into the venue. The soundboxes blared patriotic songs from Hindi movies featuring stars from Ajit Kumar to SRK. After some time, a jawan with a wireless mic in hand appeared on the road and started egging the audience for louder support and hooting of the other side. In between he would run towards the border gate. Then all the girls in the crowd were asked to come on to the road and suddenly the place turned into a disco with patriotic songs blaring. A rope was tied at a distance from the gate so that, people didn't run across the road in their excitement. Then the show began. Performed by the Border Security Force(BSF) of India and the Pakistan Rangers, the lowering of flags is a choreographed drill, speed marches and really high kicks. They stared at each other, twirling their big moustaches amidst slogan chanting. While we watched the spectacle from bench seats, there was a VIP gallery with a huge number of foreigners and other dignitaries.

Meanwhile the sun had crossed the Radcliff-drawn border to the other side, without a passport or visa and without body frisking or walking through a metal detector. Still, it did not hesitate to share its light and glory with us on this side of the border. During the whole ceremony, the guards of both BSF and Pakistan Rangers stood facing the crowds on their side, with their backs to each other. Maybe they trusted the guards of the side other side more. It was not long ago that a suicide bomber detonated himself just a few meters away from the border gate on the Pakistan side killing many.

After the flags on both sides were lowered in a very synchronised and meticulous way, there was a brisk handshake between the guards with smiles on their face before they closed the gates. Maybe they know each other since they stand guard every single day.

As the sun decided to say goodbye to all of us, we got up. The BSF jawan on the mic, requested everyone to throw all garbage in the dustbins. No one paid any heed. We all left behind a badly littered stadium and hurried back to the car park. On our return trip, I thought about the narrow line painted across the road between the two gates. How many litres of human blood did Radcliff use it to paint it? A dictator or an army general in power in Pakistan may need that choreographed drama every day to distract their citizens. But does a strong and vibrant country such as ours need to lower ourselves to their level! Is the strength of a human or nation dependent on decibel levels or staring down each other while twirling moustaches?

I am not a romantic. I reckon, the borders are a reality that cannot be wished away. Animals in the wild too mark their borders. The Voyageurs Wolf Project have published the GPS-tracked territory of 7 wolf packs way back in 2018. It is a way of nature to ensure that each one of them, whether they are single or in packs, has accesses to the resources needed for survival. Whether it is grass or prey.

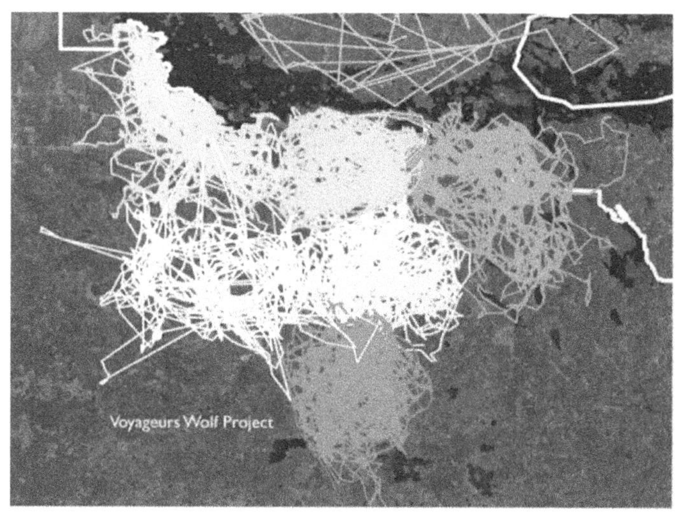

Pic Courtesy: Voyager's Wolf project

In our minds as well as in the world, we live to die and die and kill to live. When I must have a door and wall to save myself from my siblings, a fence to keep that neighbour away, and a border even within a country to say my river belongs to me, how can one have an issue with a border between nations?

Especially when that border gets written with human blood. Blood and belonging always goes together. But the moot point is, when wolves and wild animals live the way they have since they have originated on mother earth, why do we humans take pride in our evolution and progress?

The sagely phrase Vasudhaiva Kutumbakam suggests that our ancestors transcended those animalistic tendencies. The phrase Vasudhaiva Kutumbakam is made up of three Sanskrit words, Vasudhaa meaning earth/world, iva meaning like and kutumbakam meaning large/extended family. The verse finds mention in the Maha Upanishad (VI. 71-73); and is further referred to in the *Hitopadesha* and other literary works of India.

However in the current era, that sounds so archaic. Have we regressed to Neanderthal times?

Chapter 22

Recipe of Getafix's Magic Potion

17 December 2024

Is there anyone who's wondering who Getafix is?

Getafix is the druid and creator of the secret magic potion that, gives immense strength and ability to those Gauls to beat up those stupidly authoritarian Romans. He is one of the central characters of the Asterix series comics , penned by Uderzo and Goscinny. Asterix came into my life through my good friend and engineering college hostel roomie, Goofy Sudhakar Raju. Both of us were members of the Dagar gang in our hostel and were real experts at whiling away time. We always had so many interests other than engineering subjects. We both read quite a bit. I remember, we once got a copy of the novel *Gone with the Wind* just before a final exam and we both found time to read it end to end and then take the exam. During those days, I happened to procure a big poster of Obelix from the pages of *The Sunday Observer* and it adorned the wall of our room in Second Hostel. Friends started calling me Obelix and name stuck; many of my engineering college friends still call me Obelix, after all these years.

Just a few days ago, after I returned from a trip to my hometown, I told my sons, Manu and Rishi, that I wanted to send some books to Saanvi, the bibliophile daughter of Dr.Anju. Since my sons knew very well that both Anju and Appu are quite dear tome, they happily handed over their Asterix comic book collection to be shipped along with some other books. While packing the books, I ended up reading those great comic books again. It was kind of like going back to our dear room next to Partha's room in the Second hostel. Now that is whole other story.

Getafix photo courtesy: https://asterix.com/en/portfolio/getafix/

I read the following LinkedIin post the day after packing those books. It was quite early in the morning when I saw it. It was posted by an ex-partner of one of the world's premier consulting firms.

Pic courtesy: SM Linkedin Post

Under the photograph of Vinod Kambli and Sachin Tendulkar , the global think tank wrote and I quote,

"Talent+ Luck = Vinod Kambli. Talent + Luck + Discipline + Determination + Commitment + Humility + Learning ability + Off-field behaviour + Ability to digest success and failure both +Treating the game as bigger than self +++ = Sachin Tendulkar. The gap between cricketer Tendulkar and cricketer Kambli is the gap between talent alone and greatness. "

I am 54 years old and have some experience of the good, bad and ugly of the world in general, and firms in particular. My conclusion is that every facet and arena of public life do have their share of really good, good, average and so on so forth. I strongly wanted to send a blood red hot stinger reply to the post. Those who had seen Vinod Kambli bat in his prime, with those silken touches and left-handed grace and elegance, really owe him some beautiful moments. It is like G R Viswanath vs SunilGavaskar. Sunny might have scored way more runs than Gundappa, but those who have seen GRV bat still vouch for him. But then Zen practitioners practice meditation beyond the Zendo and Zazen. We try to carry the calmness and compassion of sitting meditation to walking (kinhin) to working (Samu) and then even to the rest-rooms. In fact Japanese Zen practitioners believe that toilet gods guard toilets and we have to snap our finger to request them to move on. I must mention that I was in the restroom when I read the post. So I can't let myself be less compassionate to anyone even when I'm in the rest-room.

As, it is a little difficult for me to type on the small phone screen without my glasses, and I ended up commenting , "Let us be compassionate and let Kambli be! We don't have to use every life as a tool to dish out management theories."

On reading the responses of many others, it was not difficult to conclude that many readers were in sync with that thought.

Our relentless pursuit of success has created a cottage industry of how to be successful. As a leadership and life coach who tries to make a living out of it, I too plead guilty to it. Book-shops/ the internet/ the social media pages etc. are inundated with magic potions/formulae for success. Four steps for this and six steps for that. "Walk 5 steps forward looking east, turn 30 degrees left, move forward another 6 ft , take a U-turn. And then you will achieve your success." Osho tells a wonderful story about a meeting between Henry Ford and Napoleon Hill, the author of *Think and Grow Rich*. It is worth listening to.

Secondly and most importantly, we live in a standardised world. Some amount of standardisation is necessary to keep our life simple. Like distance in cm, m or kms. Time in seconds, minutes and hours, alcohol in small, large and extra-large etc.

But when that standardisation is brought into the spheres of success, love, national pride and spirituality, then it ends up as a great disaster.

One person's benchmark for hard work for the nation is working for 70 hours per week. Someone else's standard of being a successful batsman is being a Sachin Tendulkar. And someone else's benchmark of being rich may be Ambani. No less!

Those who are sports aficionados and soccer enthusiasts still rate the Brazil football team (with Zico, Socrates, Falcao, Eder etc.) as the greatest football team ever assembled. Though they finally lost. George Best, whose life almost rhymes with that of Kambli's, is still reckoned as one of the best footballers ever played. There was even a wonderful article/obituary on him by Nirmal Shekar in *The Hindu* titled, "It was Best, could have been better".

My Zen master Ama Samy, who has been walking on a spiritual path for more than 70+ years, and whom many consider as an authority on Zen, Buddhism, Advaita and other religious streams and philosophy, may have around a few hundred disciples. And we struggle quite a bit to run our Zendo, Bodhi Sangha and do the affiliated social work we are into. That surely pales in comparison with the other "Gurus," in numbers, power and wealth! And I am sure there are many evolved individuals who lead low key and are anonymous.

The moot point here is, is there a one-shoe-size-fits-all kind of measure for success for all beings? If there is one, if everyone else becomes a roaring success and there are no failures in our world, what will be labelled as success and who shall we label as successful?

And lastly,I did ask that ex-Big 5think tank if there was a sure shot recipe for success and if Sachin had it, why he had not been able to hand it to his son and how someone like Yashasvi Jaiswal could find that recipe while selling chaats to make ends meet?

It is not just the spiritual world that is pathless land (as Jiddu Krishnamurti had famously said), even an ordinary life is indeed a pathless. Each one of us has to create our own paths and lead our own life as per our standards. Many times, regardless of our talents and capabilities, the privileges we are born with, the choices we make for ourselves and the probability of luck in this world clears or leads our way.

When we really start to live by the standards we set in our own heart, mind and soul, and when we are content with what life gives that day, and when we are compassionate and loving towards others, and we do our value contribution to the world whether it 1or70 hr/week, and take care of the needs of our and our dear and near ones (not merely the wants), and can sleep soundly at night- that is what I would call a good life. It does not matter whether someone labels it as a success or a failure.

And that is the recipe of Getafix's magic potion and my realisation.

Though in the comicstrip, Getafix, the venerable druid always says firmly to Obelix, "No, Obelix, not you!" when Obelix insists on having a portion of the magic potion!

Chapter 23

Bridge Over Troubled Waters

9 December 2024

"We've made plans to meet again. Will Paul bring his guitar? Who knows. For me, it was about wanting to make amends before it's too late. It felt like we were back ina wonderful place. As I think about it now, tears are rolling down my cheeks. I can still feel his hug."

In the1970s, widely acclaimed folk-pop duo Paul Simon and Art Garfunkel released their final album, Bridge over Troubled Water, which went on to win theGrammy Award for Best Album of the Year in 1971. At the height of their fame however, the duo broke up.

(Image credit: CBS Photo Archive / Getty Images)

With a friendship that began when they first met in school in the early 1950s, the duo catapulted to fame when their first album was released in1964. Six years later however, they threw in the towel after their final album was released.

In his memoir, Paul admits that he took offence to Art's foray into acting and Art took offence to Paul's decision to record as a solo artist early on in their career. While they briefly reunited for special and rare performances over the years, it was evident to fans and foes alike that the wounds of their ruptured relationship still ran deep.

Both couldn't deny however that when they worked together, they had the potential to create something special and meaningful for their fans. And 54 years later, an interview with Art Garfunkel last week, revealed that the two musical legends had built their own bridge over troubled water and reconciled, as the opening quotation of this dispatch testifies.

I received the above wonderfully written note from Takshashila in their newsletter Takshashila Dispatch dated 17 Nov 2024. It was a nice read and I chose to quote it as it is. Though that article's theme was AI Chip, my ordinary mind wandered into bridges that we build, burn and rebuild in the troubled waters of human relationships.

It triggered my memory about a movie I had watched as a young boy and a wonderful book I read during my youth.

The Bridge on river Kwai. I remember the storyline vaguely. How the Japanese used prisoners of war to build a bridge for war time use across the river Kwai. In the last scene, the hero who had helped, the Japanese build the bridge, ends up blowing it into pieces.

ButI have a very vivid recollection of Richard Bach's wonderful book "*A Bridge Across Forever.*"

I heard about Richard Bach in one of the Six Sigma training sessions conducted by Subroto Bagchi at Wipro. He spoke about the book *Jonathan Livingston Seagull, a*lso by Richard Bach and when I went to it from Premier Bookshop on Church street, Shanbag told me *The Bridge Across Forever* is a good book too. So, I ended up buying both. And I never regretted my decision. Shanbag was not just an ordinary book-seller, he was a true bibliophile. As long as he was running Premier Bookshop, I never ever went to another book shop.

Bridges is a great metaphor for relationships. Perhaps because humans evolving socially has a lot to do with advancement in our collective knowledge and skill of building bridges.

Many ancient civilisations started building bridges across rough and tough terrains, often in crude ways. They filled the ravines with rocks and wood so that they could cross and reach out to others. They learnt to build bridges across rivers and streams too. In the northeastern parts of India and many other parts of the world, people still build bridges using natural bamboo.

One of the oldest existing bridge in the world, that is still used by the local population is the Arkadiko Bridge in Greece. It is an arch bridge and it was built sometime around 1300–1190 BCE.

Arkadiko bridge Pic courtesy: Wikipedia Commons

When our ancestors in Greece learnt about the arch a structure that renders strength to carry a lot of tonnage, and when the Romans discovered that mortar from volcanic rock doesn't dissolve in rain and water, both findings provided massive fillip to the art and science of bridge making.

From bridges to relationships, we humans are social animals. Jiddu Krishnamurti famously said that we know ourselves only in the mirror of relationships. In my view, that includes the relationship with ourselves.

We don't have any choice about certain relationships. Those are the rummy cards dealt to us by destiny for this round of the game. We cant choose our grandparents, parents, siblings, children and other blood relatives, they just happen. Even after the initial set of 13 cards, when you get to pick your cards from a stockpile, you don't have any way of knowing that card beforehand. So, it is all about luck and destiny. We have the option of scooting and getting out of the game or staying on to play this game in this round of life. Some discard a fews cards to the waste pile, for example broken relationships amongst siblings and cousins, children abandoning their parents, parents abandoning their children etc. I too have my share of broken relationships. And then there are some who play wisely to create melds out of the available cards and win the game.

True, there are relationships where you can choose. You can choose your spouse, your friends, your neighbours (to an extent), your boss and your colleagues and clients (again to an extent). Of course you can choose your spiritual guru. In Zen tradition it works both ways. While a disciple / student has to accept the Master, the Master has to accept the disciple too. These choices are informed choices. Although, I do know now that, our so called free will is limited, yet we can exercise it to a certain extent. We can't blame destiny for those sets of cards.

In some of these relationships, we don't have to build any bridges. People miraculously will walk across water, like Jesus and Peter in the Bible, to reach out to others. Each one of us, has a Jesus and a Peter in our life. I do too. My better half Thara, my children Manu and Rishi, my best pals for life like Komal Jain and Sheik Iyer etc.

Ido have many more great relationships. Like that with my Amma, my siblings Sasi and Sandhya, my Zen Master AMA Samy, my mentors and well-wishers from childhood Dr. Radhakrishnan and Usha Aunty, late Dr. Richard McHugh, late Ranjan Acharya, Brij Sethi, Dan Pacheco, LH Rao, Ram Ramanathan , my teachers Gopala Thatha, from ALP school to APU, my bosses from R Bala to late SMR to Robert Meier, countless colleagues (especially my risk team mates from SMR's team like Guru and others.) and even clients, my friends from KTMHS (Manoj, Dr. Dinesen, Satish) to BVB (Dagar Gang) to

Wipro to Mantri Tranquil, some of my cousins and relatives. But many of them were tested in real rough waters like Jesus and Peter. Here we were all good to each other to a great extent.

But there are those who walked across water to reach out to me, and did that regardless of what I was at that point of time; or I walked across water, regardless of what they were at that point of time.

I can share an example.

A long time back, we had a friends group called Tennis Mafia, (we still have that group, though some of them have moved out of Tranquil). Some of us were good at tennis. Some of us were learning to play. A few others and I had once organised a tournament, one with prize money. During a match, Sheik and LP@HP were playing against irrepressible Erode Subbu and his teammate. I was officiating the match. Suddenly Sheik and I had a very heated argument over a point. I was fuming and stormed out of the court. I then heard Sheik saying, "Vishy you are my friend and you won't walk away, regardless of what the matter is" and I turned around. That was kind of walking over the water and reaching out. And eventually that match ended. Subbu and his teammate won convincingly. Prize money was handed our with Subbu and his teammate winning the prize. I eventually moved out of Tranquil. Life continued and so did our friendship. He remains one of those who I reach out to in hours of distress. I know I can count on him. And he can too.

Tennis Mafia @ Mantri Tanquil. Sheik Iyer is standing second from right.

I have similar stories about Komal, Thara, Manu and Rishi, and a few others too. All saved for another time. At least, I would have to wait for Komal to retire before writing his story.

In his epic *Nicomachean Ethics*, Aristotle wrote a whole chapter on friendship. He defined friendship at three levels. Friendship of utility/ transaction, friendship of beauty or power and friendship of virtue. When friendship is based on virtue, that is when people start walking over water to reach out. Even troubled waters. Even fire.

When you think about it, we can classify all our relationships around these three attributes.

One does not really need to build bridges to connect with others. Love, gratitude and compassion are the invisible mathematical arches and mortar that make it happen.

But for other levels of relationships, we may still need to build bridges. And in some very rare cases, we have to burn the bridges too. Because we know very well that those on the other shore/side won't or can't walk across the water or fire.

Chapter 24

Forgetting the Eye
and Remembering the Way

25 January 2011

Sheik "Al Kabeer" Iyer. Good samaritan, an ace tennis player and my friend. He recently got hit on the eye during a drab doubles game on a chilly winter night. The "Arabic" Iyer that he is, he returned to the court as if nothing had happened. He merely took a brief stroll outside to calm his hurt ego. When Kumar, our common friend, asked him if he could see, pat came the reply, "Yes, but through a coloured film on one eye." Hearing this, Sriram the "Intel inside" Tranquil and our no-nonsense leader of the pack directed us to take him to a doctor.

We took him to Nethradhamma on Kanakapura Road where one of our neighbours at Tranquil practiced. The good doctor was waiting for our one-eyed Sheik even though it was time for her to wind up. She was quite gracious even though it was the fag end of a long day at work. She didn't hurry us, in fact she took her time with the examination. There was a sigh of relief when she announced the good news. No major damage. She prescribed rest to the restless soul so that his body could repair the damage. Noticing his eagerness to get back to the tennis court, the doctor underlined the need to ensure no further damage to the eye while the human body solved the problem.

It is altogether a different matter that Sheik Iyer had probably the fastest recovery from an eye injury and was back at the tennis court in no time with improved eyesight and faster reflexes.

A few weeks later I happened to come across the following lines in one of the commentaries on *Tao Te Ching*.

"You forget your feet when your shoes are comfortable and only remember them when your shoes pinch."

– Tao Te Ching

"Similarly, you forget about right and wrong when your conscience is clear. You remember only when your conscience is troubled."

Human traits are quite fascinating. You forget that with which you are in harmony. You remember only that with which you are out of harmony. In my humble view, this is a good litmus test.

When a politician is on a patriotic zeal, chances are some "unpatriotic deed" is troubling him. When a religious preacher preaches on celibacy, in all probability he does not consider himself as an audience for such advice.

As *Tao Te Ching* says:

"If you are truly following the way, you forget about it; you only remember the way when you have strayed from it."

– Tao Te Ching

tWisT: There is another good quote from *Tao* (maybe meant for yours truly!) "Those who know, don't talk and those who talk don't know."

Chapter 25

Ghost of Black Panther

20 February 2023

It was one of those mornings. The sun was struggling to show up from behind dark clouds. Raindrops were still falling from the leaves. The wind carried a pleasant and earthy smell. As I started my morning walk along the narrow serpentine path through the bushes and woods of The Valley School, there was a sense of calm and happiness in my mind. I still wondered why the school didn't clear away that dense undergrowth. In a city like Bangalore, it is quite rare to have such a large school campus. It's even rarer to have allowed a forest to grow in it. Since the campus borders a forest, it was quite difficult to distinguish where the school campus ended and the forest began.

As the cottages faded away behind me into the distance, I suddenly felt a chill. Gurvinder Singh's description of the black panther crept into my mind. Many of the residents in the campus had seen the black panther. Quite grown up. One of the teachers even saw her at close quarters, when the panther was stretching in their portico. Many had seen the remains of dogs she had killed. However, the people who know a thing or two about wild animals, assured everyone that panthers are very shy animals. They don't harm anyone. I could not walk any further though the morning air was still very inviting. The last thing I wanted to spot on that idyllic surrounding was a black panther. As I hurried back to the safety of my cottage, I was sweating a bit. Every sound behind me sounded like footsteps.

One evening, my son Manu came back from school rather excited. They had spotted the panther near their classroom. He sounded quite fearless as he described how suddenly their teacher told them to return to their classroom and how one of the staff lit a cracker to scare away the feline. Once again, I felt the same chill of fear run down my spine. Every morning, I took care to remind my kids to be more alert. Not to walk alone. The school authorities had tied tins and sticks to trees. They wanted passersby to make loud noises so that the panther stayed away from the walking paths. I, for one, avoided the walk to the study center through the woods. Instead, I drove through. And every time I went to pick up my sons from the School Art Village after their evening music lessons, I kept looking for the elusive animal. The ones I saw on various online pages did not have the charm that the one I could not see had!

A few weeks ago, as we were returning from the school, my wife Thara told me that the black panther had been killed in an accident. An unidentified vehicle had hit her fatally.

I felt an indescribable feeling. It was not a sense of relief. It was a strange sadness.

Chapter 26

Gold Medal Syndrome!

1 November 2024

I was aware of this for a very long time. Almost every second coaching client of mine had this underlying root cause for most of the challenges they faced in life. One can safely say that this is quite prevalent in our current society. As I am bound by the non-disclosure clause, I thought I wouldn't write about it. This is because it would be impossible to write about the subject without mentioning a specific case study. Anything that reveals the identity of a coaching client, however remotely possible, is in violation of the sacrosanct spirit of coaching ethics. That is one of the holy grails.

But yesterday, a person I know to some extent, posted a vlog on LinkedIn about the crisis he had faced and how he successfully came out of it. The parent group that owns the IT company reposted the vlog in LinkedIn. He had been a senior leader in the company I work for and currently, he is a COO of a major IT company. What I found very refreshing was the authentic and honest way he listed the challenges he faced in his life, how he dared to take a pause from his work for a quarter of a year and how he came out of it. That takes quite a bit of personal courage. I also thought it was quite remarkable how the parent company shared his post with the world. They seem to be looking at the situation quite compassionately.

The message said, "What happens when even 'success' feels empty? COO at —-, reached that breaking point and made a choice most of us only dream of—he hit pause. No career plans, no future job lined up—just three months to recharge and reconnect. In a world that glorifies the grind, V's story is a powerful reminder that sometimes, the bravest thing we can do is to take a step back, breathe, and tend to our minds. Because at the end of the day, your mind matters."

I wrote a small reply to the post. After that, I received quite a few DMs, each seeking clarifications and guidance. This blog is in response to that.

It is very pertinent to highlight that late Ranjan Acharya—who in my view was a rare sage at a corporation—and Kayomarz Shroff recognised this pressing need of the workforce and was instrumental in initiating Mitr at Wipro a long time ago in 2002/03. It is a counselling initiative driven by employees for fellow employees. It is important to keep in mind that they started Mitr almost two decades before the current wellness at work movement. I was one of the early cohorts of counsellors and cofounder of that initiative. So, it is not that organisations are not aware of the challenge, it's just that not much has been done to change the underlying root cause.

From the title of that post in LinkedIn—What happens when even "success" feels empty? It is self-evident that mental health challenges are not just the result of empty pockets, wallets, bank balance, CV, LinkedIn profiles and meaningless and purposeless lives. Even success can feel empty. Psychologists call it gold medal syndrome, also known as Olympics syndrome. To quote, "Gold medal syndrome is a feeling of dissatisfaction and lack of purpose that can occur after achieving a major life goal." Since many super athletes seek professional help immediately after a major sporting event like the Olympics, it is also known as the Olympic syndrome.

Another closely related issue is silver medal syndrome. Silver medal syndrome is the term used to describe the tendency of silver medalists to be less happy with their medals than bronze medalists. This is because silver medalists tend to compare themselves to the gold medalists, while bronze medalists compare themselves to those who didn't make it to the podium.

All of these points to the fact that it does not take much to make us unhappy about our station in life. Regardless of who we are and where we are, it can affect our mental makeup. One's intellect, brilliance and other talents rarely equips one to manage such situations and lead one to the true path of joy and peace in life.

One response to my post read like this, "Finding that balance between hustle and rest is key, huh? Zero time sounds smart. How do you think we could fit that into daily life? "

Probably the remedy too starts with reframing that question. And it is essential to begin reframing from the word "How." Often in life, our search for a solution begins with the question "How to…" and it more often than not creates more issues and problems for us to solve. It is important to start with "Why?" To paraphrase a famous quote by Nietzsche, "He who has a 'why' to live for, will bear almost any 'how'". It points one to find one's purpose in life.

If you are one of those who doesn't like Nietzsche, then let us see what Carl Jung said. He was one of the best psychiatrists, psychologists and psychotherapists and is in fact, considered the father of analytical psychology. He said that in all his life, all the psychiatric patients above 35 that he met came with conflicts in the irreligious outlook. What he meant was that their issues stem from a lack of purpose or vision for themselves. Elsewhere he said, "Your vision will become clear only when you look into your heart. Who looks outside, dreams; who looks inside, awakes.

Let me buttress my point by quoting Viktor Frankl too, who I think knows a thing or two about surviving real trying circumstances having survived Nazi concentration camps. He writes in his seminal book, *Man's Search forMeaning,*

"Don't aim at success. The more you aim at it and make it a target, the more you are going to miss it. For success, like happiness, cannot be pursued; it must ensue, and it only does so as the unintended side effect of one's personal dedication to a cause greater than oneself or as the by-product of one's surrender

to a person other than oneself. Happiness must happen, and the same holds for success: you have to let it happen by not caring about it. I want you to listen to what your conscience commands you to do and go on to carry it out to the best of your knowledge. Then you will live to see that in the long run—in the long run, I say!—success will follow you precisely because you had forgotten to think about it."

– Viktor Frankl

This pretty much sums up the need for each one of us to have a purpose and meaning in life and that purpose must be a cause greater than the self.

Once we have the "why" question answered, it is time to step on to the path of "how"!

Recognise the Walls of Your Mind's Prison

To start with: Every human being, yes, every one of us are inmates of prisons we have created in our minds. Those prison bars and walls are invisible to our inner sight and we often mistakenly think that we are directly in touch with the world out there and are living in it and responding in it. Those prison walls and bars are made up of our own mental images about ourselves, others, and various belief systems. Unless we are aware of them, we have very little power to transcend and gain our inner freedom. Inner freedom precedes outer freedom and is essential for our peace and joy.

There is a famous quote of maverick Scottish psychiatrist R.D. Laing that is etched in my memory and I never tire of sharing it again and again and again.

"The range of what we think and do is limited by what we fail to notice. And because we fail to notice that we fail to notice, there is little we can do to change; until we notice how failing to notice shapes our thoughts and deeds."

– R.D. Laing

You will be able to transcend the prison cells of your minds only when you are aware of them. You have to realise—and not just understand. While understanding is intellectual in nature, realisation happens when you get an insight—that you don't directly live and operate in this world. You create maps in your mind. Maps or images of yourself, others in your life and the world you live in. And those maps at best are representational models of the world. Quite often a distorted, alternate factual world.

Unless you become aware of your beliefs, your mental models, and question the assumptions you make while creating them, there's very little you can do to transcend them.

Recognise Your "Wants" and "Needs"

Even if one becomes aware of the prison and can see a key, he/she has to overcome the challenge of bread. You might have seen this picture, where a prisoner reaches out to get the bread in front of him rather than the key. (Pic courtesy Facebook.)

(Pic courtesy: Facebook)

The bread is just a metaphor.And that is the second challenge. It could be a BMW or a Benz on your porch, that fancy upmarket villa with a huge mortgage, that foreign vacation, your children's desire to study in an expensive foreign university. The whole setting of the modern-day society we live in is that of scarcity and unlimited want. Scarcity is the bedrock of the pseudo discipline called economics—hope my son Manu, who is an economics major, doesn't read this—and unlimited want is our mind's creation. Nothing in nature, including your brain or heart, has unlimited want. The brain needs limited glucose and it can't handle any more glucose than what is needed. The same goes with the heart. Extra oxygen is not good for your heart. Even your body can't take in more water than needed. In fact, people can die of poisoning from too much water.

Most of our unlimited wants arise from social comparison. It is not our need. It is society's desires imposed on us. If the success of a gold medal can feel empty, so can a silver medal, bronze or no medal.

One of the keys to inner freedom is to know and be aware of our needs and wants. People can spend more than a billion dollars on a marriage and yet feel compelled to come and explain to the world why they did it during commercial time slots in a cricket match. Then you know it is important to recognise the thin line between needs and wants if you want to be on the path to peace, joy and happiness.

Find Balance

The third point is that of balance. You would have heard umpteen number of times about life-work balance or work-life balance.

We separate work from life with a solid border or wall. One has to realise every borderline is a possible battle line. Our life is the only concept out there in the world for us. Everything is just part of it. In a way, in our wheel of life, work is just one spoke. Our life wheel has many other spokes, such as, our family, friends, social relationships, hobbies and interests, social work etc. It is only when all the spokes are in sync, that our wheel of life starts rolling smoothly without any hiccups. Every spoke is important in our wheel of life if we want to lead a fulfilling life.

Now in this era of magnetic levitation and wheel-less mobility, smart minds may think of the wheel of life as a single spoked wheel. Haven't you heard that "work is life" and we need to work more and more and more?

Does Life Have to Be a Single-spoked Wheel?

Isn't it a wrong notion that life has to be single dimensional? Didn't Gandhi take time out to listen to an M. S. Subbulakshmi keerthan even when he was racing against time to get India's independence? How many know that Einstein was a gifted violinist and Richard Feynman learned to paint and play drums? Ratan Tata enjoyed flying planes and sketching. And Jack Welch truly worried about his golf scores and diligently worked on them? Did they have a lesser contribution to society in their chosen fields compared to others?

It would be interesting to read a story about one of the most successful generals the Indian Army had, "So innovative was his operational planning and so meticulous its execution that Lt. Gen J.S. Aurora did not forsake his daily round of golf even once during the 12-day battle to "liberate" East Pakistan, which emerged as Bangladesh in 1971. As India's Eastern Army commander, tasked with evicting the tyrannical Pakistani military from East Pakistan, the Sikh soldier even played a relaxed round of 18 holes inside his Fort William headquarters at Calcutta before leaving for Dacca to accept the surrender of Lt. Gen A.A.K. Niazi and 93,000 soldiers."

These are all pointers to the fact that there are many examples of great souls who excelled in their chosen field without depriving themselves of the good moments life offered them. One common denominator in all of them is a multi-dimensional approach to life.

For me the most inspirational story is that of my Zen master AMA Samy, who I get to observe whenever I am at Zendo. He is 89 years old and he still has the zeal of a fresher on his first day of work. He built the current zendo, Little Flower Zendo, when he was 86 years old. And last year, he traveled to Australia, USA and went on a long European trip, that included a visit to the icy cold Sweden, to conduct sesshins. He spends most of his waking time in meditation, meeting his students, writing or reading. It just proves to me that if one's life is aligned with the true north of one's purpose of serving others, then there are no breakdowns.

Not everyone is fortunate to lead that kind of life. Lesser mortals like me can still lead one's life being aware of ourselves, the prison cells we are in, our inner freedom and the fleeting moments of life.

How Can One Be Aware of Oneself?

Meditation helps. Meditation is not limited to what you do during a specific time slot every day. One can extend one's meditation to 24 hours, all 7 days of a week.

I personally follow the Zero minute/every hour, Zero hour/every day and Zero day/every week with a religious zeal. The life span of individual cells in our body varies, although medical science says the average lifespan of a human body's cell is 7–10 years. While brain cells last for a lifetime, the lifespan of cells that line our stomach and intestines last just for 4–5 days. Our body cells are created, lived through, they get tired and die every single moment of our life. When that is the way our body works, what is the point of earmarking a specific time of the day or a specific week of the year for rejuvenation of our minds?

It takes just a few seconds to do a zazen breath. In that one breath everything is included. Birth, life and death.

Chapter 27

T(w)o-Gether-Ness!

20 October 2024

A few weeks ago, after morning Zazen, this quote popped up in my InsightTimer meditation app. A famous quote attributed to Rumi, it said

"Tie two birds together. They will not be able to fly, even though they now have four wings."

– *Rumi*

Now, "gether" is a dialectical variant of the word "gather." The Oxford Dictionary says that "gether" as a standalone word is obsolete and its

last recorded usage dates back to the 1500s. It often tries valiantly to stick its neck out from its buried alive/incarcerated state, when we play a game of Scrabble.

I had quite forgotten about it altogether. At least consciously. But only when I began getting similar insights from everywhere, I realised that the word got etched in my brain. That's the way our minds work. We don't see the word as it is. Rather, we see the world as we are. The inferior temporal (IT) cortex is a part of the brain that decides what we must see. Suppose you recently bought a gray Suzuki Swift car. Suddenly you start noticing all the gray Suzuki Swifts on the road. That's the IT cortex at work.

I ended up reading Kahlil Gibran's *The Prophet* once again. For the nth time…

Reclaiming Freedom

I read the book for the first time before I got married. And I used a pale take from a passage to sweep Thara off her feet when I went to meet her for the first time in Mysore. "You can have as much freedom as I have in my own life. I can give only what I have. And if you want more freedom than that, you have to take it yourself." When I finished, I knew it was a YES from the 100 W bright and effervescent smile in her eyes. And that was the only time I was a successful salesman. I should hasten to add that at that point, I was not aware that although she was born with a silver spoon and brought up in a wealthy business family, her life was like that of a parrot in a gilded cage. Her father—a loving, generous to a fault, over-caring and well-meaning person—was as conservative as conservative can be, in body, mind and soul. After our marriage, on our way to Kumarakom, we landed at Kottayam railway station a bit late in the morning. While I was thinking about where to have breakfast, Thara noticed a salon just across the Kottayam railway station and got her hair cut short right there and then, while our cab driver and I waited. My stomach was growling with hunger!

That was her way of reclaiming her freedom, her life and herself.

After that I would have shared the passage on marriage from that book with at least 50 bridal couples as a wedding day wish. Just a few weeks ago, I shared that passage with a colleague, Hema's, daughter at her wedding. I remember the last para of that page as vividly as the Mahaprajnaparamita Sutra.

It goes like this:

"Give your hearts, but not into each other's keeping. For only the hand of life can contain your hearts. And stand together yet not too near together, For the pillars of the temple stand apart, And the oak tree and the cypress grow not in each other's shadow."

– The Prophet, Khalil Gibran

But even then, those scattered thoughts sprinkled here and there never built into a blog. Blogs get written not by ink or pixels, but blood from the wounds of one's heart. And this got written in my mind scape, as I drove to Bangalore from Ramapura, a small village near Kollegal, while my mother narrated her life story over four hours or so. This was last Saturday, 30 June 2024. My mother was born and brought up in Ramapura and she moved to Kerala only after she married my father. When my father passed away all of a sudden in 2006, she chose to return to Ramapura and live there, alone.

Again, that was her way of reclaiming her freedom, her life and herself.

I've heard those stories in bits and pieces many times from many people; people who are dear and near to Amma. By any yardstick, she has led a tough life. She may have carried more crosses than even Jesus Christ.

My late father too had many crosses to carry in his eventful life. May be fewer in number than those carried by Amma and Jesus. He grew up quite poor and had to start working from the age of 15 to take care of his siblings. He was honest, generous and very caring. He was very courageous too. He fought many-a-battle for people around him, regardless of who was on the other side. A local liquor baron, a cabinet minister, and others have all had to bear the brunt of his righteous fury.

One of my most vivid memories of him is of when we were living in a village named Thenkara, which was around 6–7 km away from the small town and high school. There were just 2–3 private transport buses that passed through our village during the morning school time, and many students from the community came to the town school by these buses. The buses wouldn't stop for us. And many times, my father would stand in the middle of the road to stop the bus and ensure that all the children were taken care of. I remember someone once asked him, "Sankara, are you not scared?", And he was not. He earned a good name for himself and the crowd that came home when he passed away was a testimony to the kind of life he had led.

But Amma had a different perspective about it now. She told me that when someone tries to help others a lot, some people around the do-gooder have to sacrifice a lot and suffer. And she suffered because of that.

The clarity with which she conveyed that to me just pierced my heart.

Though Amma does not read my blogs, she knows from my sister about my penchant for being a scribe of the life stories that come my way. So when I shared with her that I was writing a blog, she put her foot down and said clearly and sternly that I was not allowed to write the stories she shared with me.

Again, that was Amma exercising her new found freedom.

I left this blog incomplete until a conversation I had with a friend last week made me come back to it. When I shared my plans of moving to Zendo, he asked me whether Thara too would be joining me. I tried to explain that Thara is not into Zen and she makes her own choices in her life.

It's been 23 years since we tied the knot and we are still in love and deeply care for each other. And like two circles (enso?!) in a Venn diagram, while there are many things common amongst our likes and dislikes, there are as many things not so common. We respect each other's space and strive to ensure that the space does not shrink in any way.

Marriage is a clever institution foisted upon the fairer sex by a patriarchal society. And it often ends up becoming a gilded cage for a woman.

Even the phrase "tying the knot" signifies that. As Rumi said, if we tie two birds together, they will not be able to fly even though they have four wings.

I don't know how successful I have been in keeping the promises I made to Thara, "You can have as much freedom as I have in my own life. I can only give what I have. And if you want more freedom than that, you have to take it yourself." As in any other life, we too have had our lows and highs, ebbs and flows.

Maybe she too will share and write her side of the story some day, like my mother did!

Chapter 28

Understanding Distress and DeStress in Life

3 October 2024

Over the last few days, air and internet waves have been filled with two tragic news stories.

One was related to the untimely death of a young professional at a very well-known consulting firm and the other, a suicide at a premier management school of India. About the death of the young management professional, the reports said, "stress from a toxic workplace," while the suicide was attributed to "stress from organising The Red Brick Summit is suspected as a contributing factor!"

The first incident drew a lot of comments and opinions in social media, many of them reactionary in my view, even those from successful business leaders and public figures; while the second news did not elicit that kind of traction. The world in general, and people (we) in particular, do not have that kind of appetite for tragedy per se. Addicted as we are to Netflix and Hotstar and what have you, we want everything in episodes. One at a time.

As a primetime member of the social media mob, after scapegoating and fixing the responsibility for those tragedies in a hurry, I too was moving on. Until I observed two different ways of living and looking at the world from my teenage sons.

Before narrating the incidents, let me introduce my sons to you. Both Manu and Rishi are quite smart and intelligent, reasonably well read and worldly wise beyond their ages. And most importantly, they are their own masters. Thara and I have made it a point to let them choose what they want or need in their life. Whether it is in matters of career, education, food or even God. They also have had the good fortune of being educated at one of most stress-free, supportive, empowering and nontoxic schooling environments the current world can offer.

Manu is a second-year graduate student of economics in a premier university. He was/is very passionate about martial arts and has represented his university team in an intercollegiate Taekwondo tournament. I was attending a sesshin at Zendo while he was at the tournament. When I did not see any message from him for two–three days, I was a bit worried. I was relieved when he called me one evening. He narrated quite happily how he cleared four tough rounds and lost in the quarter final. To quote his own words, "Papa, he was too fast and good for me, and I got pummelled a bit and I will take a day or two to recover. But my coach told me I did well, and I've got to be ready for the tournament at IIT Kanpur and I've got to practice. Am going there."

As a parent, I was quite happy and proud to hear that. Not many things can be as stressful for a youngster as an intercollegiate martial arts tournament. What more can a parent, a life coach and Zen teacher aspire from his son than the way young Manu took a physically hurting (and possibly mentally too) defeat in his stride, and was looking forward to his next stint at the arena.

But that pride did not last too long. Just two days later, Thara called me to say that Rishi, our second son, who is in the 12th standard, seemed to be a little stressed and was having trouble sleeping. And that was a complete surprise for me. I had considered myself as one of the coolest cucumbers in the world as a student. I had shared quite a few times with my children, how as a final year Mechanical Engineering student in 1994, I chose to watch all the world cup soccer matches held in the USA and chose to skip quite a few exams. Due to the time differences, the matches often started early in the morning. My roomie and good friend Goofy Sudhakar and I used to be the only two idiots in the hostel TV room. Sudhakar stopped being my partner in crime once his favourite team Germany lost. But I continued valiantly until Brazil won the final against Italy.

Rishi is one up on me on the coolness quotient. He is the kind that will wait even if someone raises an alarm that the sky is about to fall on his head. So the news about him being stressed was a bit amusing for me. I suspected some romance in the air when I spoke to him after I came back home. After completing his two-week internship at the Rahul Dravid Academy, he talked a bit about joining a sport management course and said that his dream job was to work for ManUnited, his favourite team. But he had not applied his mind on how to reach his goal. And that would have hit him now, especially when he heard the clear-cut plans of his hostel mates about what they were going to do next year. He realised he did not have any such plans yet. Perhaps for the very first time in his life, my son was worried and stressed. He managed to hide that within himself until it started affecting his life and behaviour. Fortunately for him and us, we noticed the changes in time and could help him out. All it took was a 5–10 minute "Reframing the perspective" exercise that Thara and I had learnt from the venerable NLP Guru Dr. Richard McHugh some 20 years ago. That did the trick and soon he was back to his normal self. The very next day, Tuesday, I had to wake him up so that he wouldn't miss his bus to school and his term examination.

I'm not trying to say that the world we live in, including environmental factors, don't play a role in making our lives miserable and stressful. They do. But the real villains are the three pounds of human cells behind our eyes and between our ears. Nature/God/natural selection/evolution have ended up designing how we humans survive. They don't care if we are left scared, fearful and miserable, as long as we last one more day in our account of life and manage to pass on our genes to the next generation. That is their common minimum program and nothing more. We're all wired and programmed for it.

To quote from one of the foremost modern texts on the matter:

> *"The individual's perception of environmental demands and personal coping resources is the critical variable in determining the nature of the stress response. The objective conditions of the environment are important only to the extent that they influence these processes of primary and secondary appraisal".*
>
> *– Evans and Cohen on Environmental Stress*

That is written in academic English for psychology professionals.

But from my Epistemology classes with Prof. Indrani Bhattacharjee at Azim Premji University, I know that is no different from rajju-sarpa-nyaya of Indian philosophy. As per that idiom, when there is less light, a curled up rope is mistaken for a snake. And that happens due to the inbuilt programming nature has written inside our skulls leading to fright and fear and anxiety. But when the light returns, calm and peace comes back due to the accurate perception of it being a mere rope. And the gap between de-stress and distress is approximately 23.7 mm. That is the sagittal vertical (height) of a human adult eye.

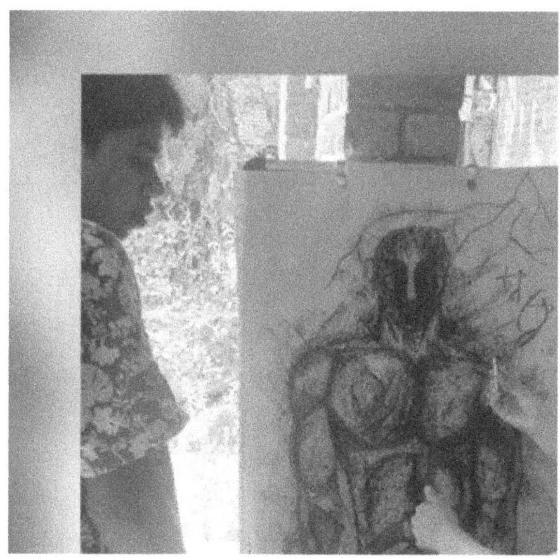

No wonder the Buddha, Siddhartha Gautama, the noble one, chose Samma Ditti (right view) as his first core teaching in his eight fold path to wisdom. And we will-be able to perceive this reality as it is only when we are aware of the programmed filters nature has put in us, with which we look, hear and feel this world.

Even if the "rope" is a real poisonous snake, remember that Stephen Covey's quote,

"It isn't the snake bite that does the serious damage; it's chasing the snake that drives the poison to the heart."

– Stephen Covey

Chapter 29

The Spoke of Work in the Wheel of Life

26 November 2024

Sometimes, the metaphors that are most commonly used indicate how we have been conditioned to think.

I have two points of view regarding this thought.

First about the term "Work–Life balance."

The term work-life balance triggers the image of a weighing scale with two trays that separate life from work. It is actually more helpful to imagine life as a wheel with multiple spokes. They are the spokes of our relationship – with ourselves, with our dear and near ones, organisation and society, and also how we take care of ourselves (exercises for mind and body), recreation and entertainment, silent time, work etc. Each spoke is as important as any other spoke, if we wish to keep the wheel of life rolling smoothly, without toppling to one side while travelling on the way of life, we must remember that each spoke is as important as any other. Along with the spokes, the spaces between them are just as important. And each spoke is a relationship we have with one facet of our life. All those spokes consist of what can be called living. We cannot take living out of our life. Likewise, you cannot take out of those spokes out of the wheel. (Though the concept of maglev was invented by a German engineer more than a century back.)

As Lao Tzu wrote

> *"Thirty spokes share the wheel's hub; It is the center hole that makes it useful. Shape the clay into a vessel; It is the space within that makes it useful. Cut doors and windows for a room; It is the holes that make it useful. There benefit from what is there; Usefulness from what is not there."*
>
> *– Chapter 11 Tao Te Ching Lao Tzu*
> *(Translated by Gia-Fu Feng and Jane English)*

If we let any one of the spokes out grow other spokes, then the wheel or circle ceases to be one and there ends its journey in the way of life, temporarily or permanently. Then it is not just about over working, people can get negatively affected by over exercising or overeating or say binge-watching Netflix as a way of entertainment. There is a limit to how much glucose our brain can take or how much oxygen our heart can take. More or less is not only not beneficial, it can be very harmful.

Secondly, it is important to note that certain professions, need utmost focus and attention and such intensity can be sustained only for a few hours at a stretch. It could be the role of a surgeon, a truck/bus driver, a pilot or even a cook. Each one needs a break from work so that and the body and mind can rest and get rejuvenated again. But for many other professions, that is not completely true. However if people think they need a complete segregation of work from the rest of their life, it probably indicates, that the environment in which they work contributes to their stress rather than the work itself. It could be a toxic work culture, a toxic boss, or overly competitive coworkers etc. Speaking about myself, if I am not too to keen on finding out, or i am annoyed or feeling stressed out about why my Boss or work colleagues or my clients are trying to reach me , when I am immersed with other spokes of my wheel of life, then it could stem more from their images that I have created in my mind. Images that i am sure not too positive. We could reverse that question and check our sentiments. If a loved one, tries to reach us during our work hours, what would be our response?

To take this argument forward, iff someone still thinks the spoke of work has to be separated from his wheel of life, s/he needs to think deeply and evaluate, whether that particular spoke fits in their wheel of life in values and principles. I agree that each one of us has a different wheel of life. While I still consider my wheel of life to be that of a bullock cart, there are people whose wheel of life is like that of a Ferrari.

Chapter 30

Zen, Manu, Rishi and Mastercard

12 December 2024

Yesterday I shared the news about my decision to leave home and and live at the zendo with many people. Thara and Rishi had a holiday due to the death of a prominent politician and Manu was home for his vacation. My younger son, Rishi suggested," Let us treat Papa to dinner at Paragon" and we set out for Paragon @ Church Street for an early dinner. He knew my favourite restaurants in Bangalore are TRC and Paragon.

After placing our order, as I looked at Manu and Rishi's faces and listened to their discussion, what came to my mind was what Gibran wrote in *The Prophet*. I wonder, how many times I have read that small book. At least 100 times for sure. Though I can type in most of the verses from memory, let me quote from the text.

On Children

And a woman who held a babe against her bosom said "Speak to us of children"

Your children are not your children They are the sons and daughters of life's longing for itself They come through you but not from you And though they are with you yet they belong not to you

You may give them your love but not your thoughts For they have their own thoughts You may house their bodies but not their souls For their souls dwell in the house of tomorrow

Which you cannot visit, not even in your dreams You may strive to be like them But seek not to make them like you For life goes not backward, nor tarries with yesterday

You are the bows from which your children As living arrows are sent forth The archer sees the mark upon the path of the infinite And he bends you with his might

That his arrows may go swift and far Let your bending in the archer's hand be for gladness For even as he loves the arrow that flies So he loves also the bow that is stable

Courtesy: Wikipedia

With Thara, my better half.

A long time ago, Thara's grand uncle, who was a very wealthy coffee planter in Wayanad, visited us in Bangalore. He suggested that we send our children to Rishi Valley School. He himself had his school education at Rishi Valley before the Second World War and then went to UCLA for his graduation. When Thara said that it would be too expensive, he very generously offered to pay their fees. Apparently, even after Thara completed her engineering , he offered to fund her higher education in the USA. But her conservative father could not even imagine his daughter studying in such a faraway place. Maybe I am the fortunate one, ror I would not have met her!

We moved to Kanakapura Road from BTM Layout, so that our children could go to a Krishnamurti school. When we went for Manu's interview-the school interviews parents and not the children to ascertain their fitment to the school's purpose and culture-Dr. Satish Inamdar, who was then the director of the school, told us that - you have got to let go of your child, just as a mother bird let her young ones fly away. Your son may end up as a great artist or an ordinary painter. In a way, he was advising us not to project our own life aspirations on our children. It was quite sage-like advice, and he said it like a prophet.

Years later, as Manu was considering his post school options, as a matter of a fact, he told me and Thara, "while I appreciate what you both are, I really don't want to belike you. I want to be rich, and I want to be an investment banker.". He wanted to further pursue his education in financial engineering and is currently enrolled in an Applied Economics degree at O.P.Jindal Global University. Last week, he taught me about options and futures in simple terms, I was all ears and my heart was swelling with pride and admiration for him.

Rishi is at the opposite end of the spectrum. He draws and paints well and I suggested that he should take up fine arts. But his mind is focused on sports management and he even spent a few weeks at the Rahul Dravid Academy.

Rishi with Rahul Dravid. Or is it the other way ?? :-)

He is the one of the foremost fans of Manchester United (ManU), and wants to be involved in Sports Management. His craze for ManU might have started after I got him a few original football jerseys while I was working in the Gulf. The first one was a ManU jersey. I jokingly told him that I would work hard to finance his MBA in Sports Management so that he could work for Liverpool Football Club instead of his dream with ManU. I asked him how could I, a Liverpool fan, finance a potential employee of our rival Manchester United! I urged him to switch sides. And Rishi with a brave face, told me, "Papa I don't need your money, I will apply for a sports loan. But I am going to work for Manchester United. And that was that.

By then our food arrived and the discussions changed.

While we were waiting for the bill, Thara shared a recent news story of Ananda Krishnan, the Malaysian tycoon who passed away just a few days earlier. It seems, his son left a $ 5 billion inheritance to be a Zen monk in a monastery at the age of 18. Now he is an abbot in that monastery. Rishi then asked me, "Papa, aren't you too leaving a billion dollars each, pointing to Manu and himself?"

I could respond with a wry smile only. After paying the bill with my credit card I said silently to myself, "There are things money can't buy, like Manu, Rishi Thara and Zen. For the rest, there is Mastercard."

Truly Grateful

I would like to express my sincere gratitude to:

Thara, my better half (in all respects) and significant other, and our children Manu and Rishi, who are so much wiser, more loving (than me). They have always just let me be. My Amma who is spiritual without any religious trappings and who still worries about her maverick son, and my siblings Sandhya and Sasi. I was the middle child in our family, so they took care of me from both left and right. AMA Samy, Zen master, founder of Bodhi Sangha and Little Flower Zendo, Perumalmalai, Kodaikanal, who is my sage and guide on The Way. Rasna Baruah, editor par excellence, who took up the challenge of transforming my scribbles into readable passages. Late Ranjan Acharya, who some 15–16 years ago, replied to my email with the message that, "the only way to become a writer is by writing", and Komal Jain, my anamcara friend, who goaded me to pursue writing more earnestly. And readers who belong to the Dear and Near group on my phone who always read the first uncut copy of my blogs and who put up with my writing and still encourage me.

Lastly, to all the Buddhas—past, present and future—who walk/ed along The Way.

About the Author

Vishy Sankara is a student of Zen Master Fr. AMA Samy at Kanzeon Zendo, Perumalmalai, Kodaikanal and is a Zen teacher. He is also the Administrator of the Zendo and Secretary of Bodhi Sangha, a Zen community. He makes a living (or tries to :-)) as a as a Life Coach (https://mindzendo.coach) and Management Consultant (Change and Transformation). He is an avid blogger (https://kokorozendo. life) and is an "aspiring" writer. He lives at Kanzeon Zendo (https:// kanzeonzendo.in) with three Zendogs: Bhim, Birdie and Wuji.

Birdie and Wuji, Tai Chi masters checking out Francois's Tai Chi steps, while Bhim is not interested…

Epilogue

I have been a lover of words from a very early age. My heroes in life were / are writers like O.V. Vijayan or Kamala Das. And it takes a lot of courage to claim that one is a writer, when one still looks up to them. At the least, I don't make any such claims. I have been blogging for some 15 years and I ventured into this at the behest of my good friend Komal Jain. It started with the idea of earning a few more Rupees for myself, when I was out of a job, but by the time it reached the form of a book, I ended up as a Zen monk. Now at this point of my life, I don't look forward to earning anything for myself now. But when "we" cease to exist as we have done so far, the world fills up that "empty space " (Mu / Wuji). Now I work for the Zendo and the social projects undertaken by Bodhi Sangha trusts. We run a school for the underprivileged at Perumalmalai along with a number of social interventions to lessen the suffering of many. Your contribution towards this project will be utilised for a nobler purpose. Also on the anvil: Zendo Chronicles and A wayfarer's guide to Zen. Seeking your mind share, heart share and soul share.

www.ingramcontent.com/pod-product-compliance
Lightning Source LLC
Chambersburg PA
CBHW041320120726
48005CB00014B/2064